Fables, Fantasies and Folklore of the Isle of Man

Fables, Fantasies and Folklore of the Isle of Man

Harry Penrice

The Manx Experience

Published 1996 by
The Manx Experience
45 Slieau Dhoo, Tromode Park, Douglas, Isle of Man
IM25LG

Chapter and book jacket illustrations by Alan Perkin

ISBN No 1 873120 26 5

Printed by
Alden Press, Oxford

CONTENTS

The Author

HARRY PENRICE loves the Isle of Man! He was born inPort St Mary and lived in various parts of the Island eventually residing in Sulby Glen. His involvement with the woollen industry caused him to move to the textile county of Yorkshire and later to settle in Derbyshire. His relaxation from business was spent walking over rugged hills, bleak moorland and the entire Pennine Way. This provided the material for his articles published in various outdoor magazines and his book "Daily outings on the Pennine Way".

His wanderings did not lessen his affection for the Isle of Man and the highlights of his leisure time were still holiday visits 'back home', part of which he spent wandering over the wild and relatively deserted Manx hills. In common with most Manx folk he developed an interest in local folklore and the tales of country dwellers and he has now coupled this with his interest in writing

Fairies at the Bottom of My Garden

THE Isle of Man is steeped in mythology and folklore and although books may tell of the Island's origin as the ice cap moved northwards, what really happened is much more romantic and interesting.

In those pre-history days there were two opposing giants who lived in Ireland and Scotland and they were constantly quarrelling in a rather violent fashion. In one of their more extreme fracas they were having what the Manx children call a sod fight, throwing clods of earth at each other. The Scottish giant made some particularly rude remark and the Irish giant furiously responded by grabbing an extremely large clod of earth. He was a little over ambitious. The cavity which it left almost immediately filled with water and formed Loch Neagh and the large piece of earth fell short of Scotland and splashed down in the Irish Sea. That sod today is called the Isle of Man and has been the home of the little people, fairies, goblins, bugganes and the phynoderee from its unexpected beginning to the present day.

Manx folklore starts with Manannan, who was the son of the sea, and his wife Faud. Manannan was a magician and Faud was an enchantress and they ruled the Island as priest King and Queen. It was probable that prayers were said and sacrifices made to Manannan from many of the stone circles that can still be found on the Island. About 500AD the saints visited and drove out Manannan and Faud but up to that time they had kept the people happy, and secure, united and free from invasion.

Manannan had three forms of defence. He could throw reeds on the water and they changed into ships and each ship became a hundred ships, so no one dared to invade the Island. Even the Romans, in their four hundred years of mastery in Europe, dared not invade against this magical fleet. Secondly, he could conjure up the clouds to lie low over the Island so that strangers could not find it, and thirdly, he could change himself into a wheel of fire. Then he would roll over the mountains and into the glens to terrify and destroy his enemies.

When he was driven out by the Christian saints he yielded up his kingdom but he did not lose his interest in the Island or all of his power.

He still brings down the clouds, known as Manannan's mantle, to protect the Island from any visiting royalty. Fire can still be seen streaking down the hillsides in winter storms and his voice can be heard roaring in the glens. His wheel of fire lives in perpetuity and is symbolised by the Manx crest of three legs which stand whichever way they roll. It lives also in the more recent Millennium crest of a three spoked wheel to commemorate one thousand years of parliamentary rule.

There are still lots of fairies in the Island but the increased population and modern developement has made it hard for them to get about, especially as so much iron and steel is used. These are elements that the fairies can't fight and so they hide in the rich vegetation of the Island, in the straw in barns or in the apple orchards of country cottages.

This is exemplified by the account of the poor Manxman who wanted to marry the daughter of Illiam Christian but was being rejected by her parents because of his poverty. One night he strolled into his orchard and saw a fairy burying her fairy gold under an apple tree and, when she had left, he went and dug the gold up. He was now rich and he showed his gold to Illiam Christian who then gladly gave his consent and the young lovers were married. On the night of the wedding there were great celebrations and the groom crept out into the orchard hoping to see the fairy with more gold. When he got to the tree he saw the fairy crying and he felt ashamed of his greed. He apologised but explained that he had to have the gold so that he could marry the girl he loved.

It seemed that they had only been talking for a short while when the fairy told him to go back to the house. As he walked in he was surprised to see a strange man sitting by the fire and his bride, in everyday clothes, preparing two young children for bed.

With a look of dismay she cried, "Where have you been? Seven years ago, on our wedding night you walked out and never came back. Now I have married another and these are my children."

There was another fairy who took the form of a human woman. She was extremely beautiful and nakedly she rode a horse through the countryside. Her beauty was like a magnet to the young men and they followed her. Laughing she rode her horse into a deep river and the bewitched men still followed her. Six hundred were drowned. The fairy queen was very angry and she punished the fairy, her horse became a porpoise and it still dives and gambols off the coast of the Island. The fairy became a wren and it hid in a thorn bush and every St Stephen's day the children parade with a cage on a stick and sing "We'll hunt the wren."

The White Lady of Caraghyn was another evil fairy. She lured the menfolk to her bedroom with music and song. They spent one night of bliss in her company and returned to their former haunts as old men having lost a full lifetime of human living and had only a few short weeks of dying in which to remember their one night of heaven.

Of course all these spells could be broken with a bit of iron or steel, or a pinch of salt. When the steam railways came to the Island and steel rails were put down and steel engines ran all round the south, out to the west and up the coast to Ramsey it made things very difficult for the fairies. Then the electric railway ran up the east coast, with sparking wires, and even went up to the top of the mountain and the fairies found that there were few places where they could hide.

There are fairy men on the Island too. They are known locally as the "Li'l Fellas," some are mischievous but generally speaking are harmless. If a housewife is kind to them and leaves them the odd jar of buttermilk she will often find them helpful and will get up in the morning to find the fire lit and the housework all done. Those who disbelieve are likely to have poor health and sickness, their crops may fail or even well-washed dishes will become soiled while still stacked away. Crockery will mysteriously get broken and kitchen fires refuse to light. Should the disbeliever be a visiting holiday-maker the chances of a happy fine holiday are nil and wind and rain will force them indoors for much of their stay.

Bad fairies have even been known to steal babies from their cots or to stop the new mother's milk, but all this can be avoided by hanging a little cross of rowan twigs on the back of the door. The twigs must be carefully broken from the tree when the sun is shining and must not be cut or trimmed with a steel knife because steel is offensive to the little people.

One day a farmer from Malew was going back home from the mart at St Johns, having had a drink or two in the Tynwald Inn. Up over the top of Foxdale he wandered into a fairy hall where hundreds of fairies were dancing with a lot of humans. He immediately recognised some of these men as former neighbours who, he thought, had left the Island and gone across the water to work. A lovely little fairy danced up to him and offered him a flagon of wine but as he raised it to his lips a man said, "Hold it, boy, if you drink that you'll become one of us and you'll stay here for ever."

The farmer, remembering some of the fairy folklore, quietly slipped to the back of the room and tipped the wine on to the floor. He was ready to sing a hymn or say a prayer but he found that wasn't necessary. There was a huge flash of light, his head spun, he felt himself falling through space, the hall and all its occupants disappeared and the farmer found himself sitting in a deep ditch by the roadside.

One of the bigger fairy men of the Island was known as the Phynodderee, which means the hairy one; he was very big and strong and would do a variety of things for kind people. One time, to help a poor farm labourer in Sulby, he carried all the stones from the shore to the glen and helped to build a house. The farm labourer was rather shocked by the Phynodderee's unclothed hairy body so he presented him with a suit made of good woollen cloth. This offended the fairy man who went away crying, but after that every time the farm worker tried to light his fire the thatch roof was burned off.

Another fairy man was the Doeiney Oie and he lived on the east coast near Laxey. Whenever a storm was going to blow up he would make the most fearful howls that would reach all the little inlets, cottages and nearby farms and the fishermen and the farmers would take heed. Crab or lobster pots and nets would be hurriedly raised by the fishermen, boats would be securely moored and farmers would round up their animals until the storm had passed.

The Glastyn, the horseman from the sea, was not so kind. He rode out of the sea at night on his white horse searching for pretty young maidens who would be charmed into riding on his horse as pillions. He would then return to the waves and the maidens would be lost forever, but his mission had to be completed before sunrise and the cock crowed or the girls would return safely to their beds.

The most unpredicatable of all the Manx spirits are the Bugganes. These were quite numerous evil spirits that lived in the wild and wooded area and they would descend in the dead of night to dance in the fields and if the mood took them to damage crops, scare animals and even destroy buildings. One such instance was when St Trinian's church was being built at the foot of Greeba mountain. The buggane didn't favour the establishing of a consecrated building on his playground so he repeatedly blew off the roof of the church before it could be consecrated.

A good fairy told the local tailor, Tim Kelly, how to overcome the buggane's badness. The secret was that the tailor must sit in the church throughout the night and between sunset and sunrise he must make a complete suit from a bolt of homespun cloth. As the sun set Tim spread out his cloth and busily plied his scissors. Throughout the night Tim snipped and sewed and dawn was getting near when the angry Buggane dashed into the church screaming, Tim was just sewing on the last button, but in fear he dropped the suit and fled over the hill to Marown church knowing that the Buggane dared not follow him on to such holy ground.

The frustrated Buggane dashed back to St Trinian's and in anger tore off his own head and threw it through the church door. It rolled down the aisle and rested on the unconsecrated altar and burst into flames. The almost completed thatched roof was blown off in flames and to this day the church stands deserted and roofless and the Greeba Buggane has never been seen since.

There are lots of other spirits, some good some bad. The Keimagh sits in the churchyard to guard the dead, allowing them to rest in peace. In such places as Spanish Head and Gob-y-Deigan the Ceightagh lives in the caves and talks to the shellfish and other marine life. The Croghan crouches like a frog in the bottom of most wells ensuring the water remains sweet and fresh.

It is difficult to separate the Manx spirits from ghosts and no one is certain into which category the Moddey Dhoo should be placed. He was the large black dog that lived in Peel Castle. When the castle was a fortified garrison the soldiers always went about in pairs for fear of this monster that lived deep in the dungeons and would prowl around the keep. One night a young soldier was made brave by a drop too much from the bottle and he volunteered to go alone on his final rounds to lock all doors.

Shortly after he left the guardroom a most frightening scream echoed through the castle. The rest of the guard, sensing a disaster, went en bloc to investigate and found their young comrade badly mauled with teeth and claw marks over his entire body. They carried him back to the guardroom, a raving madman. He never regained his sanity.

Much later in Manx history another strange spirit registered itself in the west of the Island. It was Geoff, the Dalby spook, who claimed notoriety in the 'thirties. Geoff was a talking mongoose. There is no record of him ever doing any real harm but he secreted himself behind panelling at an old farmhouse at Dalby and would impart a variety of imformation about impending happenings and arrivals. This mysterious creature was almost a confidant of the young daughter of the house and was always more talkative when she was present. If annoyed he would break dishes and throw things across the room, but if pleased would chatter in foreign tongues and mimic visitors to the house, but always remaining unseen by any member of the public.

Another story of the 'thirties relates to the fairies that lived near Ballalona Bridge. An Englishman had purchased a farm nearby and openly stated that he would sow corn in a field that contained a fairy ring. The locals were very concerned and asked him not to as this was where the fairies danced under the full harvest moon, but he persisted, stressing that the field had lain fallow for long enough. In due course the corn was sowed and months later he was boasting about the terrific crop that was standing ready to be mown. Mowing would start the following day. During the night the countryside in that area was filled with strange noises, a perculiar roaring sound came in from the sea and swept over the farm although the Island, as a whole, was calm. When daylight came the corn was battered and bruised well beyond possible harvesting and in the middle of the field was a perfect circle. Battered corn was trodden into the ground as if by a thousand tiny dancing feet.

Ballalona Bridge is also known as the Fairy Bridge and it is courteous to raise one's hat when crossing and say "Good Day, Little People." During the 1939-45 war there was a Fleet Air Arm base in the south of the Island and the pilots, acknowledging the Little People, would regularly salute. The Commanding Officer heard of this pactice and condemned it as superstitious and barbaric and posted an order stating that it must cease forthwith. The pilots complied but over the next two weeks a couple of aircraft were mysteriously lost over the Irish sea. The C.O. revoked the order, the pilots saluted the 'little people' and safely took to the air.

The Isle of Man has had, and still has, its share of witches. In recent times there was a Witches Mill at Castletown where covens gathered and spells were reputedly cast. It is claimed that all modern witches are not evil but this was not acceptable in years past. Near the centre of the Island is St John's, the site of Tynwald Hill where on the 5th July the new laws are promulgated. Slieu Whallian overlooks this historic site and was the location of an old anti-witch ritual. The suspected witch was taken to the summit and placed in a barrel with knife-like spikes on the interior. The slopes are now tree clad but in ancient days they were relatively bare and the loaded barrel was rolled down the steep slope. If the occupant was still alive on reaching the bottom she was declared a witch and had to be destroyed by fire. It was a hard life for would-be witches.

In modern times witches are not likely to be treated in this cruel manner, but they probably do not cast evil spells and are content to live quietly in the countryside relishing the beauty of their chosen home.

* * * * * *

INTERMISSION

The foregoing information comprises some of the tales that have been passed down by folklore or, in more recent times, by gossip and word of mouth. Most Manx people can recount many of them but the following stories are figments of imagination only loosely built on odd factors that have come out of the fables, fantasies and folklore of Ellan Vannin.

The Author

* * * * * *

Halloween Challenge

"SURE an' 'tis a brave man y'are Bobby McMeiken, sailin' across there in the dark, it'll be near to dawn when y' get there. It's Hallowe'en y'know. The devils are about on this night."

Bobby laughed. He had just dropped his catch of herring at Ardglass and was setting sail for Peel in the Isle of Man. He looked at the grey autumn sky and the stillnes of the water as it lapped against the harbour wall, the peaceful serenity of this Irish village was so like his own home that he longed to be off. There was a pleasant southwest breeze coming off the land - it would be a calm fast trip to his native island. He looked with a sense of pride at his boat with its solid workmanlike lines. He'd skippered her since she slid off the slides at the old shipyard on the banks of the river Neb. She was one of the last boats to be built there and every item had been hand-crafted and assembled with pride.

He calmly jumped from the quayside into his boat. "I'll be home and in bed before my fish are in the shops in Belfast if you fellas don't move a bit faster," he jokingly said. "Come on John, let's get going."

The cables fore and aft were cast off and hauled aboard and the *Rowan Cross* silently sidled away from its moorings. Bobby and his small three-man ketch knew these waters so intimately that a glance at the sky, in either day or night, and an inborn sense of seamanship was all that was necessary to guide his vessel over the forty odd miles of open water. Night had settled and it was still dark as he edged the *Rowan Cross* alongside the concrete steps of the breakwater at Peel. The tide was too low to take her to her usual berth in the harbour, it would be another two hours before that could be achieved with safety. The black skeletal groyne which stretched out from the harbour jetty was lit by a single red lamp and the low water exposed minor sandbanks near to the harbour entrance. The small town across the bay was in almost complete darkness, here and there a faint light gleamed where a fisherman was on the move either returning home or preparing to leave.

The entrance to the harbour was dominated by the red sandstone castle, built on St Patrick's Isle nearly a thousand years ago when it was separated from the Isle of Man by a narrow strip of water. In years past a narrow causeway had linked the small island to the main island at low tide but that had been replaced by solid concrete and now a good quality road ran from the town round the harbour to the end of the breakwater, and St Patrick's Isle was no longer an island. The buildings within the castle walls had long since lost their roofs and gaunt walls reached skyward. The curtain wall still proudly stands intact and encompasses almost the entire islet being breached only at the gatehouse where there is a massive heavily studded door.

The castle, as with all age-old castles has its share of folklore and legend and the Moddey Dhoo, or Black Dog, features largely in the history of Peel Castle. No one living has actually claimed to have seen this ghostly creature but there have been mysterious disappearances over the centuries and some have claimed that the Moddey Dhoo has sated its appetite for human flesh as a result of these lost souls.

Bobby and his mate, John Greggor, in their blue jerseys and turned-down seaboots climbed the steps up to the breakwater.

"Come on," Bobby said, "let's walk round the harbour. Young Kinley can take her up single-handed in a couple of hours. I'm dying for a decent pot of tea and a bite to eat."

As they looked towards the castle, homeward bound, John drew back in fear.

"Oh Holy Gawd," he gasped. "Look at the lights, the devils are about tonight."

His hand probed deep into his trousers' pocket searching for the little crucifix that Jenny had given him after the 1929 storms. It had kept him safe for three years and he sought its comfort once again as greenish blue lights seemed to dance over the ruined walls of the castle. He was sure it was something evil and demoniac and bode ill for anyone who approached.

"Oh that! 'Tis nothing," retorted Bobby. "A bit of a cloud, sea mist or something, and a bit of light from the moon."

"But there is no moon, there's no light in the rest of the sky. 'Tis the Moddey Dhoo and the devils. It's Hallowe'en and it's evil. Let's stay on the boat, Bobby, we have the cross made of rowan on the masthead, y'know that'll protect us from the devils, witches and the like."

Bobby snorted with disgust. "Aw, that's a load of rubbish, if there were such things what good would a bit of a twig do, no matter what tree you got it off?"

"Y' shouldn't talk like that, Bobby. I know my grandma, and her's before her, always used the rowan cross to keep the devils away, an' my gran lived to be a hundred. And if you didn't believe in such things why did you call your boat the *Rowan Cross* and let me put a new cross on the masthead each year? I've got one hanging on the back of my door at home and I bet y've got one too."

Bobby ignored the arguments being put forward.

"Aw don't be an old woman, John," he said, "y'don't really believe all that stuff, do ye? There no such thing as the Moddey Dhoo - a big black dog - it's just stupid. That story's five hundred years old, and it was all imagination then. No one has ever seen this dog. When I see it I'll believe it. Come on," he held out his hand, "hold my hand, boy, you'll be safe enough."

Shame made John step forward but unseen by his skipper he was grasping his crucifix and silently repeating the Lord's Prayer as they walked along the breakwater past the round fort and the lifeboat house and then followed the curtain wall towards the castle entrance. John hung back as they passed below the castle walls, he anxiously glanced at the heavily barred entrance to the crypt, that was where witches and devil worshippers had been imprisoned centuries ago, but it was in darkness. The old cathedral above was equally quiet. Devils there may be, he thought, but they haven't invaded the holy ground yet, although that evil glow still persisted over the decaying walls of the old gatehouse and that had always been considered the haunt of the Moddey Dhoo.

Nearing the steps leading up to the castle entrance Bobby danced forward. "I'll call him out," he yelled as he dashed into the dark entrance of the gatehouse and banged on the heavy studded door.

"Moddey Dhoo, Moddey Dhoo, if you're there come out and show yourself and let an honest fisherman go home to his bed."

The huge door swung open and Bobby tried to turn but unseen forces pulled him forward. He saw a vast room with scores of ill-formed canine creatures, some with dog's heads on misshapen human bodies, others with the reverse. Their hideous human heads had gaping screaming mouths but their bodies were dog-like and covered with long black hairs. They scrambled and fought each other, snarling and screaming in anger, fighting to reach their goal and oblivious of Bobby who was being drawn into their midst. Their goal was a huge black dog to whom they appeared to be paying homage, but this was no ordinary dog. It stood erect in an almost human stance, its long black hair gleaming in the light of a mysterious ball of flame that floated over its head. The dog's huge body was grotesque and repulsive but its dazzling bright red eyes were like magnets drawing Bobby forward. Saliva drooled from its wide open mouth and its fang-like canine teeth were smeared with blood. A head-bursting cacophony filled the room and Bobby could feel the perspiration trickling from his brow into his eyes. He wiped it away with the back of his hand and his hand was smeared with blood. Cold winds seemed to swirl around the room and yet his body burned and hot blood ran into his eyes. His brain fought against the supernatural attraction that was drawing him towards the frightening monster that stood below the ball of light and he could feel his feet unwillingly shuffling forward.

John gripped his small golden crucifix bravely holding it aloft and loudly chanted his creed.

"I believe in God the Father, God the Son and God the Holy Ghost," he yelled as he dashed up the steps and grabbed Bobby by the arm. They stumbled down the worn sandstone steps and the great door slammed shut. The gatehouse was still illuminated by the spectral green lights that moved incessantly over the ruined walls and the air was filled with the lamenting howls of a thousand hounds.

Bobby broke clear of John's faltering grip and plunged into the chest-high water in the harbour, scrambled up the ferry steps opposite and then fled along the shore road seeking the sanctuary of his cottage.

Fear had given Bobby inhuman strength

and speed and John stood dumbfounded, still holding his crucifix and chanting his creed, as he watched his skipper flee with a strange floating ghostly light mysteriously sitting over his head. As the figure disappeared, the spell was broken and John ran round the harbour always looking towards the water of the incoming tide or the silent town beyond, but never towards the devil-haunted castle.

For two full days Bobby lay on his bed in a shivering semi-conscious state while his terrified wife watched his features change. The doctor was called but he casually said, "He's had a shock, his pulse is normal, so is his breathing. He'll be all right after a little while, just let him rest. That'll be seven and sixpence please."

But it was a different world for Bobby. It seemed that his life had started when the castle door swung open and the large black dog took control fixing him with that gory stare. Every time he opened his eyes he saw the black dog, its malevolent blood red eyes piercing his very soul. He looked at the window set close below the eaves and the dog was there, on the window sill, the eyes sending a dreaded message. He looked at the door - it was there; it was on the dressing table or in the corner, always there capturing his soul and his brain and wanting his body. He closed his eyes and shivered.

On the third day he had stripped off his flannel nightshirt and was curled in a foetal position on top of the bed clothes. Mary noticed the dense black hairs that were sprouting on his body and limbs and she threw a blanket over him to cover his nakedness. He growled and moved exposing the long curved claws that had replaced his workworn and broken nails. As his lips were drawn back in a snarl she saw fang-like eye teeth, which seemed to be visibly lengthening, and bloodlike liquid was drooling from his mouth and staining the counterpane that covered the bed. Mary put the plate of food on the floor and fled in terror to kneel and pray in her kitchen.

The creature lying on the bed upstairs was not her Bobby; he had always been kind and gentle and she'd welcomed him back when he'd dashed into the house in a frenzy and thrown himself on to the bed. She knew there'd been a calamity of some sort and she tried to placate him. She'd gently removed his wet clothing and shrugged him into his flannel nightshirt, then she'd tried to climb into bed to comfort him, to hold him to her bosom until he was ready to unburden himself of his worries, but he had ordered her out. As she had stood by the bed it almost seemed like a dog's bark as he'd repeated the harsh words, "Out - out - out!"

On that third day, grabbing an old coat, she ran up the street and banged on the door of the Greggors. A tear stained Jenny answered and they fell into each other's arms.

"Jenny, is John in, is he all right?" cried Mary.

"He's in but I'm frightened," was the heart-rending reply. "He ran in three days ago, when they came back from Ireland, and threw himself into bed. His eyes were staring wide open and he kept repeating the Apostle's Creed. He won't let go of the little crucifix that I gave him three years ago. But why are you here? Has the same thing happened to your Bobby?"

"Oh Jenny, it's terrible. He's in our room and he's changing, he sent me out. I dare not go near him. He's becoming some sort of a beast, he isn't a man anymore. He's not the Bobby I married. The doctor said he'd had a shock and that he'd be all right. He didn't do anything but he charged me seven and sixpence. God, I would give a hundred pounds and my life to make Bobby what he was before."

I think your Bobby is in a worse state than my John," said Jenny. "The doctor said the same to me and he didn't do anything, just said to keep him warm. But I do think that John is getting a little better, he had a little broth today, I had to feed him like a child, I think he tried to smile, but I daren't ask him what happened. We'll just have to pray that they'll both be all right and perhaps they'll tell us what happened when they're better."

"Aye," said Mary, "we'll pray."

She went back to her cottage with a little hope and a lot of dread.

When next Mary went upstairs and cautiously entered the bedroom she found the plate empty. It was pushed into a niche by the dressing table with scraps of food scattered around and the knife and fork unused. Her husband was on all fours crawling round the room, sniffing at the wall and furniture. He growled threateningly as she peered into the bedroom. His body was taking on animal-like proportions but his ungainly movements were neither animal or human. His actions were so unnatural that they would have been amusing if they had not been real and being performed by the creature that had developed from the man she had once loved.

The facial features were semi-human but the glaring blood-red eyes and the canine teeth made it hideously repulsive. The room reeked of unclean animals and Mary opened the widow to release the stench that was spreading through the house and then ran in fear as the animal sprang towards her with bared fangs. She heard it scratching at the door which she had slammed behind her. She retreated to the front room and found her well-worn Bible and dropped to her knees and prayed that this nightmare might end.

For days Mary listened to strange noises coming from the bedroom. With dread she would climb the stairs and slide a plate, piled high with food, towards the bed. A hideous frightening growl was the only response and she would stumble unseeingly and frightened towards her kitchen. She no longer prayed for the return of her husband but for freedom from the monster that now occupied their marital bedroom.

Seven days later there was silence, there was no response when she rattled the door handle. She cautiously opened the door a few inches and peered through the gap, the plate of food was untouched, but she dared not enter. It was after another twentyfour hours of silence that she forced herself to enter the stinking room. The bedding and curtains were torn to shreds and had been shoved into a corner to make a bed. The old well-worn furniture was scratched and broken, the walls and floor were covered with filth. She cautiously stepped forward, looking into the corners and under the bed, but there was no human nor animal occupant.

In the days that followed Mary burned the

old furniture and repeatedly scrubbed the room but the smell remained. It was an evil odour that gradually permeated the entire house so Mary locked the door and left.

* * * * * *

John doesn't go fishing anymore. He can often be seen standing on the quay or even the harbour jetty opposite the castle, but he always has his back to the castle, looking towards the church, with a Bible in his hand. On Sundays he goes and prays for the soul of Bobby McMeiken or any other soul that is in torment and he thanks Jenny for her little gold crucifix.

Mary's cottage still stands empty. The windows are grimy and the frames are rotting for lack of paint. Slates have slid off the roof and are left lying in the garden that no one tends. Odd balls and other toys have fallen there and are left unclaimed, even the very young children sense the aura of evil, and the brave young braggarts from the quayside would not venture to walk on Bobby McMeiken's ground.

They have moved Bobby's boat to a deserted spot at the top of the harbour. The paint is peeling and the name is almost indecipherable. The rowan cross has disappeared from the masthead, decay and dereliction are taking over. No one visits the old boat and the children do not play on the discoloured deck.

It has been said that a large black dog was seen prowling and sniffing round the hatches and the midship fish hold, but no one has really challenged it to show itself.

Now at Halloe'en, at the fateful hour, one can sometimes hear a dreadful howl of anguish coming from the ruined castle and an echoing plaintive call from the deserted *Rowan Cross* slowly rotting at its moorings.

TARRO USHTEY

THE forlorn looking cottage clung precariously to the steep slopes of Cronk ny Arrey Laa, the undraped windows looked out over the lonely blue sea. Deserted heather clad slopes stretched from the top of the precipitous cliffs to rugged rock outcrops on the ridge of the mountain. As the rain-bearing southwest wind swept in over the Irish Sea and grey clouds settled on the peaks, its loneliness was emphasised. It was such an insignificant abode that it had never been given a name and was referred to as Rob's place. Rob had been born there, in this little hovel that his father, also called Rob, had built and Mary had come as a penniless bride just before the father died.

The inside of the cottage offered no comfort. Part of the floor was formed of rough slate slabs and the remainder was beaten earth. A rough wooden shelf held a few chipped and discoloured dishes and a rough table and crude stools completed the furnishings. On each side of the fireplace were bags of heather covered with coarse blankets and a blackened pot hung on a hook over the smouldering peat fire.

For most of the day Mary could be seen scratching at the small clearing of unproductive soil behind the house struggling to raise a few vegetables that could go in the pot. Her young son, Ewan, would often be by her side or down on a small green patch a few hundred yards away where a scrawny looking cow was searching for blades of grass. The little lad was bare legged and shoeless and had a wild strange look in his eye. The few people that had met him had claimed that he was a strange being, able to talk to the huge herring gulls that swooped over the cliffs and to the peregrines that nested in the rocks above. He was small and delicate and his skin hung loosely on his small frame, but that was expected as his mother and father, and even the cow, were equally emaciated.

Each morning before the first rays of the sun had touched the mountain top and the western slopes, with its lonely cottage, were still in darkness, Mary would stir from the bags of heather that served as a bed and blow a bit of life into the embers of the fire to prepare a cup of weak tea and cut a crust of bread for Rob to start his day. He would then climb those steep slopes to reach the Glen Rushen lead mines and start his days work. For hours he would delve into the bowels of the earth, often knee deep in water, to haul out a few barrow loads of heavy grey rock. Through the years his skin had become the same colour as the metal he sought and his hacking cough retched up sputum of the same repulsive colour. For this daily toil he received a few shillings a week which barely covered the cost of their scanty clothing and the few essential items of foodstuff, such as tea and sugar, that they couldn't produce on their small patch of soil.

The cow had been a gift from a sympathetic farmer. It was a miserable looking animal, its feet were malformed and its legs splayed out from the body. The locals that saw it called it a Tarroo Ushtey, and said that it had been sired by the spectral water bull that was reputed to come out of the water and ravage the crops and perhaps mate with one of the farmer's cows. Rob had some doubts about accepting the gift but Ewan pleaded with him. The farmer lived some four or five miles away and Rob had taken Ewan with him to consider the gift. There Ewan looked the beast in the eye as it lay against the hedge and immediately it rose on its spindly legs and walked towards him. The lad spoke gently in words that were unknown to his father or the farmer and then they turned for home. The Tarro Ushtey calf followed with no further coaxing, no stick, rope or barking dog was necessary.

And so the little animal settled at Rob's place. It could usually be seen on the small green patch but some days it was inexplicably missing and then Ewan would sit on the edge of the cliff and look longingly out to sea. The next day it would be back and the boy and the beast would be contented once more. As time passed it grew and developed and Ewan would collect a jug of milk in the morning and again at night. The cups of tea became more palatable and cooked food using the milk augmented their sparse menu and slowly their bodies gained a little weight.

But it seemed that there was a price to pay for this new found sustenance. Ewan spent more time with the animal and would sometimes be missing for the whole of a day and a night, but when he came back he would always be happy and contented. When questioned he was vague and didn't appreciate that he had been absent.

Curiosity prompted Mary to spy on him and she saw her son, who was still small and light despite the extra years, mount the animal's back and grasp the horns. He spoke words that were unknown to her and the beast responded with a muted roar. It turned towards the sea and gently picked its way down a narrow track, little more than a rabbit run, until it reached a pebbly cove. With no hesitation the creature moved to the water's edge and stepped bravely into the foaming brine. The water swirled up round its belly and Ewan's feet dangled in the water. It went on until only its horns were showing and the boy was slowly submerging. The water closed over Ewan's head and Mary wept. She cried for her quiet, strange little son and returned to her cottage in agony.

The sun was setting when Rob returned from work and Mary told her tale of woe. Together they went to the edge of the cliffs and looked at the sea. Sparkles of silver and gold danced over the waves but there was no sign of their son. They ventured to the small track that the animal had used but the way was so narrow and tortuous that they dare not go down the cliffs to the sea. They cried themselves to sleep and yet life, such as it was, had to go on. It was a sad, despondent Rob that climbed the slopes to work and a dejected Mary that scratched the earth up round her few struggling vegetables, but as the sun got higher in the sky she looked towards the green patch - and there was Ewan. The cow was there searching for its morsels of grass and Ewan was sitting close by unconcerned about his overnight absence.

These absences were not a regular occurrence. Maybe for one night every two or three weeks his heather bed would be unused. His dish at the table would be untouched but he never returned hungry and he never said where he'd been. Mary and Rob could see that now, although he was quiet and strange, he looked stronger and healthier. Clothes that had hung loose were now bursting at the seams. He talked strange words to the cow but he spoke with a touch of wisdom and confidence to his parents though never did he discuss these submarine visits.

Even the added milk in Rob's diet could not overcome the water and the lead that were undermining his health. The cough became worse and the climb up the hill robbed him of all his strength so that when he arrived at the mines he was unable to fill his quota of barrows. The fear of dismissal added to his worries. How would they manage without those few extra shillings that were placed in his cap each Saturday? Mary and Ewan shared Rob's worries and each went their own way for solace. Mary struggled in her vegetable plot while Ewan sat with his cow.

That night Ewan's bed was empty but when he returned the following day he went straight to his mother. In his hand he had a bundle of wet brown weed. It was slimy to the touch and smelled of the sea. "This is for Dad," he said, "put it in his broth." It was said with such authority that Mary did not question the instructions and she prepared a special dish of broth for Rob. Immediately he had eaten it he went to sleep and Mary and Ewan gently moved him to his heather bed. Not once during the night did he cough. The dawn came and he drank his cup of tea and ate his bread and set off with boundless energy up the hill on his way to the mines.

From then on it was usual for Ewan to make regular trips to the sea and each time he brought back a handful of weed, sometimes it was green, others brown or yellow, but always with the same briny smell. They all had broth that contained some of this new ingredient and their health improved, their bones no longer protruded through sagging skin. Rob could do the work of two men so his masters paid him half as much again as he'd been paid before and they revelled in their added gain. Mary worked with new vigour in her vegetable patch, and weed was brought from the depths of the ocean to fertilise the land and her garden thrived. She harvested her crops. She and her family were happy, they were well fed.

The autumnal rains were of exceptional severity; miniature ravines were gouged out of the mountain side and streamlets cascaded down the steep slopes and sprayed over the cliff edges. Heavy black clouds settled over the crest of Cronk ny Arrey Laa but the family felt secure in their rugged little cottage. Rob threw another turf on to the smouldering fire and settled on his heather bed with the coarse blanket covering his fully clothed body. Mary, similarly clad, snuggled close for warmth, and Ewan slept soundly across the hearth.

The rain beat down incessantly and Rob could hear the cow gently moaning as it sought shelter in the lee of the house. It was a strange restful sound and combined with the melody of the storm it lulled Rob and Mary to sleep. As the night reached its darkest hour a gigantic roar seemed to come from the mountain and the ground shuddered. It was as if the earth had absorbed all the water possible and the soaked peat with the heavy subsoil was breaking away from the rocky core of the mountain. The earth below the rocky crests split wide and, with a further groan, slid down the hillside.

The frightening sound was heard in Dalby and Glen Maye to the north and Fleshwick and Port Erin to the south. The roar reached over the mountain top to Ronague and over the Plains of Heaven to Foxdale and towards Peel. Later when people saw the vast landslide they said the roar was a cry of pain by Mother Earth as a great wound was created in her surface. But the old men and women with knowledge of past demons said that it was the Tarroo Ushtey calling its progeny to return to the safety of the water.

As the slide had broken away from the mountain it had slowly gained speed. The cottage heaved and moved intact but then, almost disdainfully, was turned aside. It no longer faced the sea. Its door hung lopsidedly, one hinge broken. The small windows had lost their glass and the single room was full of silt and sludge. There was no sign of life.

It was three days before distant neighbours visited Rob's place and found the uprooted cottage. There was a smell of death, and brave men armed with shovels cleared away the vast quantities of soil and rocks. They found the bodies of Rob and Mary, still on their heather bed, but there was no trace of Ewan. The vegetable plot, the small patch of grazing and cow were also missing.

Many years have passed but the cottage at Rob's place still stands askew. The door still hangs on its single hinge. It is an eerie place. The few animals that graze on the slopes never approach the building and humans would not willingly pass through the door. Through the years it has stood empty and deserted, the grass round the walls is brown and shrivelled and no weeds have grown in the traces of soil that still cling to the floors and walls. Now, if you dare to enter, you will find the room cold and forbidding, the cottage is empty but you will feel that you are not alone. No animal ever enters but you will find an odour - the sour pungent smell of cattle combined with the salty smell of the sea. If you find a morsel of moist seaweed, then you are fortunate. Take it home and put it in your broth and all your ailments will disappear.

Standing at the cottage and looking north you may see a small string of rocks stretching out from the headland at the Niarbyl; many claim that, when the moon is high, they have seen a cow-like creature,covered with greyish-green weed browsing on those rocks. A small human creature sits upon its back. It is Ewan and the Tarro Ushtey.

Mist on the Mountain

AS Colin looked out of the cottage window at the pleasant sun-dappled reservoir he knew that the past night could have been really disastrous if it had not been for the kindness and knowledge of the old lady. It was his own stupidity and lack of experience that had landed him and the two boys in such a perilous position. Being a single parent family made life very hard and he was, at times, too anxious to please the boys by agreeing to their wishes.

Yesterday afternoon had started pleasantly enough with a scramble up the hillside. His plan for the day had been to climb up the lightly wooded slopes of Sky Hill until they reached the mountain fence. Then it was open moorland with purple heather and low, ground hugging gorse bushes covered with bright golden flowers. It was heaven after the drab streets and near slum conditions of their home in Salford. He wanted Peter, who was nine, and Neil, seven, to enjoy nature and he had sacrificed a lot of personal luxuries to finance this island holiday.

He had been told that an obvious track would lead him over the hills with clear views of the fertile plain, with its patchwork of fields, stretching from the main Ramsey road through to the Point of Ayre. Beyond that, on a clear day, would be the blue Irish Sea and in the distance the mountains of Scotland.

"In jus' a little while you'll get a track down to Block Eary, it's a small reservoir, and down to Sulby Glen. That'll be a nice li' walk and the's buses back into Ramsey."

It all sounded so easy, they would be back at the boarding house for their meal at six o'clock and the fresh air was certainly giving the boys great appetites. But they had really taken to the open country and they were ambitious. Peter had spotted a pylon on the top of Snaefell.

"Dad, what's that thing on the top of the mountain," he shouted as he bounced along a hundred yards ahead. "Is it to show the highest point."

"No, not exactly," replied Colin, "although it is the highest point in the Island, but it's actually a radio mast so that people on the ground can talk to the men in the aeroplanes."

"Let's go there," he called back, "it would be a smashing walk and we'd be able to see what was on the other side."

"Oh, it's too far, we'll miss our dinner, we have to be back for six otherwise you'll have to go to bed hungry."

"We wouldn't, y'know, we could get some fish and chips if we're too late for dinner, anyway Mrs Corlett would keep some for us," argued Peter.

Colin tried to reason with him. "I'm sure it's too far for young boys like you. You'd be very tired before you got there, climbing those steep slopes, and then you'd have to walk all the way back. I don't think we should try that today."

But then Neil joined in. "Please Dad, we won't be tired, we've walked a long way before."

As they both pleaded, Colin argued. He knew that it was too much both for him and the boys but he wanted so much to keep the boys happy and help them to have a memorable holiday that he finally conceded.

"O.K. then, but don't blame me if we get lost," he said with a chuckle. "You know it's a long way and I haven't got a map."

"We don't need a map to find our way to something we can see," said Peter. "It'll be easy, come on, Neil, we'll show Dad the way."

The two boys happily danced ahead and Colin followed. It was approaching five o'clock when they reached the summit and were greeted with the most fabulous view. The whole Island was spread out below them and the blue sea surrounding it sparkled in the sunshine. They settled into a small hollow and shared a small block of chocolate before the boys dashed off to explore and Colin, thankfully, settled back against the soft turf and closed his eyes. This was worth coming for; he dozed with mental pictures of small green fields and rolling hills, blue sea and white powder puff clouds tumbling through his brain.

Suddenly he felt a chill wind and opened his eyes. It was unbelievable. The blue sky had gone. Instead low clouds swirled overhead, the base of the pylon was clear but white mist concealed the top. Colin anxiously called the boys, pleading with them to hurry but even before they were ready to leave, the base of the radio mast was also in the clouds and soon they could see no more than ten yards in front of them. Snaefell was a menacing wilderness.

They started down the hill, going in the direction that Colin imagined would lead them towards that small reservoir that had been quoted as a landmark. He realised just how inexperienced he was in these conditions and how foolish he had been to fall asleep with never a thought for the safety of the young boys or himself.

"We'll just keep going downhill," he said, "We may not end up in the right valley but we'll get out of this cloud and then we can see where we are. I think I saw a road down there when we were on the top of the mountain. Perhaps we'll be able to get a bus."

The trio scrambled down the mountainside. The boys were more subdued now. There had been a noticeable drop in temperature and there were no paths to follow. They were forced to scramble through furze, heather and low, dense gorse. This had looked beautiful in the sunshine but now the gorse scratched their bare legs, bits of heather got into their shoes and unseen holes made walking difficult. After about an hour of uncomfortable walking they reached the road that Colin had seen but to his dismay he found it was narrow mountain road and he knew that no buses would travel on that road. What was even worse was that he didn't know where it led to or where it came from.

"Are we going to wait for a bus?" asked Neil.

"I don't think we should, it might be a long time, or there might not be a bus along this narrow road," his father replied.

Neil sobbed. "But you said that we'd get a bus when we got to the road. I'm tired, I want to go on a bus."

"I really think we should keep walking, boys," pleaded Colin.

Peter joined in. "Let's wait for the bus, Dad. Please. My feet are sore and my legs are scratched and I'm tired too."

Colin's resolve weakened. He didn't know what to do and he knew that the boys were tired and he felt the same way. "All right," he said, "we'll wait here half an hour and see if a bus comes but if it doesn't we'll just have to walk on. It'll be getting dark soon and we can't stay here all night."

They huddled together for warmth and Colin told them stories, but no traffic came along the road so in half an hour they moved on. This road was completely unknown to him and as it ran fairly level he decided that he would follow his original intention of heading downhill, so he crossed the road and headed down the fairly gentle slope towards the valley. At least he felt that they were getting out of the damp mist but it was getting dark and they were all feeling cold and depressed. Every few yards the boys were demanding rests and both were crying and Colin was so dejected that he also felt near to tears. His one hope was that they would find a building, an occupied house was too much to hope for. Eventually they reached a small stream but there was no sign of any road or even a path.

He looked at his watch. It was almost ten-thirty and they were lost. He had been carrying Neil for nearly an hour and his legs were beginning to ache. Suddenly a figure loomed up out of the gloom; it looked like an old lady. She came closer and he saw the old-fashioned bonnet which put her face into deep shadow, a heavy black cape and a long black skirt that was sweeping the ground. He felt that she must be old and a recluse to dress like that; he'd only seen it before in pictures of Victorian times. But despite her apparent age she moved easily as she came to his side.

"Give me the little one," she said. "You're tired; where are you going?"

In some way she exuded safety and comfort and Colin unhesitatingly handed Neil to her. She opened her cloak and held the child close with the cloak closed round him.

"Sleep child," she said, and he, without a murmur, settled against her body.

"We came up from Ramsey," said Colin. "then we went up to the top of Snaefell and got caught in the mist. I'm afraid we're lost. We're tired and cold, we'd like to find a house but any building would be welcome."

"There are no houses up here," she said. "But you come with me and I'll take you to some shelter where you'll be safe and can rest till morning. 'Tis a dark night, the heavy clouds are hiding the moon."

Colin didn't hesitate. "Oh thank you," he said, "that's what we want."

The old lady moved off. She didn't seem to plod or stride, she just moved easily through the furze. Colin thought how nice it would be to be able to move like that through this rough country, it appeared so effortless. She was dressed like an old lady, her voice was that of an old person, everything indicated age and yet she moved with ease like a young graceful girl. She held Neil under her cape with one arm and Peter had automatically moved up alongside and taken her other hand and yet she didn't falter or stumble.

"Come, Father," she said, "put your hand on my shoulder to steady yourself; it'll ease your tired legs."

It was incredible. Immediately Colin touched her cape that felt so cold and clammy he felt his legs lighten. It was strange the coldness seemed to be leaving his body, his hunger was disappearing and his feet didn't stumble. It was amazing how easy it was to walk when he was by her side with his hand resting on her shoulder. She must have walked these mountains for years to have acquired this skill.

They were climbing slightly. Without any distress, they crossed a road but Colin didn't know whether it was the same road or not; he didn't care, he was content to put himself completely in the hands of this wonderful old lady. She was so completely confident. She moved as if she knew every stick and stone, every bush or tussock, every hump and hollow. To have questioned her goal would have been unforgiveable. Colin knew that she was leading them to absolute safety. Not a word was spoken and their quiet footfalls, as they moved over the rough vegetation, were absorbed by the damp clouds and the darkness of the night. They had not gone far from the road when the ground fell away into another valley but the pace was the same effortless glide. He glanced at his watch, it was a quarter before midnight when the clouds lifted and moonlight filtered through and he could see a deep valley ahead. As they descended a rough track, some farm buildings came into view and Colin sighed with relief.

"There's hay in the barn," the old lady said. "The little one's asleep."

Colin had forgotten Neil. This old lady had carried a seven year old child in her arms for over an hour and had still had the energy to help Peter and him along. They went into the barn and both children were laid in the hay. Neil didn't waken and as the old lady bent over and touched Peter's eyes he gave a weak smile, immediately his breathing changed and he too was asleep.

"I will go home now. I live in the valley," she said, and Colin watched her glide down the farm lane in the same effortless way.

It was just twelve o'clock when Colin looked down the valley. The weather had changed, clouds raced across the sky and the full moon cast grotesque shadows that scurried across the valley. He could see an expanse of dark water, which gleamed intermittently in the splashes of moonlight, a road or farm track with odd little paths leading off. He thought he saw the old lady on the road, or was it a shadow? It passed through the hedge and went towards the water's edge - and then a dark cloud covered the moon. When the light returned the road was empty and the dark water gleamed.

When morning came he tidied himself and the boys as best he could. The lads were amazingly spritely and bubbling over with enthusiasm. It was strange they didn't seem to remember the hazards of last night. Sleeping in the hay, in a barn, had been a great adventure and they chatted as if it had all been planned.

"Can we do this again, Dad?" asked Peter, "I liked sleeping there, it was so warm and now we're right out in the country and there's nobody but us. We can have lot's of fun round here."

Neil wasn't going to be left out. "I liked it too, Dad. None of the other boys at school have slept in a barn." He felt that this experience put him well ahead of all of his school friends. "If we didn't go back we could live in the old house that's just over there."

They stood at the barn door and looked at their beautiful surroundings. It was obvious that the boys were fully recovered from their experiences of last night. Colin decided he wouldn't say a word about getting lost and the old lady's kindness. If they had forgotten it all so quickly he didn't want to revive any unpleasant memories. As he pondered over this Peter was thinking of more practical things.

"Dad," he said plaintively. "where are we going to have breakfast, I feel very hungry."

"I'm sure you do," said his father. He knew they'd had nothing to eat except a bit of chocolate since lunchtime yesterday. "Come on, we'll walk down the road and see if we can find a house. There must be people round here to look after the reservoir. Country folk are always kind so I'm sure we'll be able to get something to eat. It won't be a cafe but we'll still be able to pay for our breakfast."

The boys needed no second bidding at the

mention of breakfast. They were through the gate and down the road away ahead of him as usual. The little white-washed cottage looked so homely and the lady of the house was so kind and friendly. When she knew that they had spent the night on the mountain, had slept in the barn and had no breakfast she couldn't do enough for them. Real country breakfasts of salty bacon and fried eggs, thick slices of bread and toast dripping with butter appeared as if by magic.

"Don't rush," she said. "Sit and talk awhile, I always say there's no rush because there's all tomorrow untouched. It's nice to have a chat and to see a strange face occasionally. You don't live on the Island, I can tell by your voice. Will you be staying over here long?"

Colin knew that she was probing for information and wanted to know why they were on the mountain and how they had found shelter in the barn, but he decided to say nothing about the old lady.

"We're just on a fortnight's holiday," he said. "We like the mountains and the open country. It's so different to home, so yesterday we set out for a walk up into the hills. It was a smashing walk and we got to the top of Snaefell but then we got caught in the mist and lost our track. We were lucky to find the barn and we couldn't see any houses so we slept there, and now we really appreciate your hospitality. Could you tell us just where we are, it's all strange country to me?"

"Bless you, yes. You're at Injebrek, you've just passed the reservoir. But it's mighty easy to get lost up on the tops. The mist drops so quickly, it's Manannan's mantle, they say it drops on the hills to protect the Island from royalty. Y'not the King of England, are y'," she said laughing.

"No, we're nothing like that," was the reply. "I wish I was, then I wouldn't have to save so hard to pay for our holidays. But thanks for telling me about the mist, we will watch it more carefully in the future. We've got another week yet and we want to see as much of the Isle of Man as possible and the boys love the wilder spots."

They sat and talked, the boys fed the hens and played in the garden and she told Colin tales of country life. She proudly showed him a christening shawl that had been used by her great-grandmother and the spinning wheel on which the woollen thread had been spun from their own wool. Then Colin noticed a photograph hanging in a darkish corner. There was a lady standing at a cottage door. It was sepia coloured and rather faded so he knew it was old, but it was the clothes that made the impact. People didn't dress like that anymore but he had seen garments just like them. It was just like the old lady who had helped them last night and although at no time had he got a clear view of her face he felt sure that this was very similar.

"That's a nice picture," he said, "who is the lady?"

"Aw, she was my husband's Aunty Ellen," was the reply.

"Does she live near here?" queried Colin.

"Bless you, no. She died, must be forty or more years ago. I don't recall her, but my husband does. He used to talk a bit about her, but there's not much talk of her now. It was a sad tale really. Poor old Ellen."

"Why is it so sad?" asked Colin. "She looks a nice enough person in the picture."

"Aw well, the poor soul died in the asylum over at Braddan. She never got over losing her little boy, y'see."

"I like to hear these local stories," said Colin. "I wish you would tell me about it, if it doesn't upset you too much."

"No, doesn't worry me. It used to worry my Tom. People said some nasty things when the old woman died in the asylum, but y'know she wasn't really mad. Years back Ellen was a fine looking woman and a good wife. She lost her husband early in life, but she was tough. She had a little boy to bring up on her own and there was no wage coming into the house. Ellen didn't give in and she was too proud to beg off anyone. She knew every inch of the mountains, she'd helped her husband with ditching and fencing but she couldn't do work like that on her own. All her life she had used the herbs and berries from the mountains and she managed to get enough money to live on by gathering herbs and things for herself and her neighbours. She'd even go to Douglas on a Saturday and sell them in the market. Her little fella was always with her whether she was on the hills or down at town.

"He was a lively little soul an' when he got about five it was a mischievous little imp, aw, the devil was in him all right. He would hide from his mother and she would come looking for him and then he would jump out and try to frighten her. One day they were up on the slopes of Snaefell and a sudden mist came down. As you know it happens pretty quick. Ellen lost the little lad. She stayed up there all night looking for him, calling his name. It was unusual for them to be gathering so far from home and she didn't know his hiding places, but she struggled through till morning searching and shouting. She came back home and the neighbours went to look for him. They found him two days later. He'd fallen down a hole. One of the men spotted the greybacks circling over the spot, but the birds had found him first an' had taken his eyes. Ellen carried him home in her arms; oh, she was strong, but the child was dead. The grief and the moon got her, she never got over it."

"What do you mean the moon got her?" Colin asked.

"Well, the moon was full at the time but it was hidden in the clouds and after that, especially when the moon was full, Ellen would wander round the mountain all night. She said she was looking for lost children. As she got older they took her away. T'was for her own safety really."

"Where is her cottage?" Colin asked. "It is such a sad story I would like to see it. She was a good person and obviously a devoted mother."

"Oh dear, you can't see the cottage now," she said. "It was way down in the valley and no one lived in it after Ellen was taken away. Of course they've built the reservoir since then so it's under the water now. They say things stay as they are under water so I suppose it's still there."

Colin had a mental picture of a kind old lady gently laying his two boys in the hay and a dark shape moving down the road, through the hedge and into the still water. He knew the cottage was still there. He had seen Aunty Ellen going home last night by the light of the full moon, her mission completed.

Lady in White

JAMIE climbed on to the bank from the little fishing boat and slipped the rope round the old wooden post. His father, aboard the ketch tightened the rope with the old hand windlass and *Manx Maid* was secure for the night. The old man had sailed these seas for the past forty years, starting as a boy of ten and Jamie, his son had followed the same pattern. He was now twenty and would in time take over from his father. The *Manx Maid* was considered one of the fastest small vessels sailing out of Castletown and for six days a week would be plying between the small ports of Ireland, England and the Isle of Man.

The Island was following the lead of the mainland. Already they were laying steel tracks from Douglas to Port Erin and soon steam trains would rush along those tracks pouring out clouds of black smoke. Many people thought that in the near future people from the southern towns would take their produce to Douglas to be sold in the market that had been established down by the quay. Some even thought that the days of sail may be limited and that even small boats would somehow be fitted with engines and paddles. Jamie's mind didn't dwell on such fanciful thoughts; he was more interested in the past.

He had loved the castle, that overlooked the harbour from his childhood and he had spent wonderful hours scampering round its passages and cells. He knew practically every stone of its structure and had often sat spellbound while the old men told tales of its ghostly past. There was one particular story that intrigued him. It recounted how unsuspecting folk had wandered into secret underground quarters and, over the centuries, hundreds of souls had disappeared into this dark unknown and had been unable to discover the way out. However, one brave individual intentionally entered but had equipped himself with a spool of linen thread. The story claims that he visited several large caverns or chambers underground and only retreated when he encountered a giant armed with a huge sword.

The story remained with Jamie through his childhood and he had sworn that some day he would venture into those subterranean passages. He had searched for and discovered the concealed entrance and on one quiet summer evening he decided that the time was ripe for his exploration. With a reel of knotted fishing lines he quietly slipped into the passage.

It was dark and tortuous and as he progressed he carefully laid out the thread to guide him back to daylight. After struggling for about twenty minutes he saw lights ahead. There he found that the story was partially true. He was in a huge cavern. He couldn't see the roof when he looked up. It was like a pitch black sky but ahead he could see what appeared to be a very stately mansion. The windows were all lit with numerous candles and paths ran up to the door. He nervously crept up and peered through a window. The huge room with sumptuous furnishing was filled with people in fine clothes. They appeared to be dancing but Jamie could hear no music. He was tempted to enter but he glanced down at his well-worn breeches and rough footwear and faltered. He couldn't mix with such fine folk.

He quietly slipped away from this fine house and headed further into the unknown. The next cavern had the same dark overhead dome but the area was filled with light although he could not see the source of this illumination. The area represented a village green, grass stretched as far as the eye could see and in the centre of this vast meadow there was a fountain with a jet of water which reached towards the unseen ceiling and then spread out to fall in a beautiful silver shower. Scores of young men and fair maidens were dancing in and out of the water. They were all fully-dressed in gay clothes but strangely as they passed through the water they did not appear to get wet.

Jamie looked in amazement. He was sure that the young folk were laughing and talking but he could hear no sound. It was such a happy scene that he had a feeling of well-being and contentment. He looked into the faces of the young people and as their eyes met Jamie heard voices and laughter which seemed to come out of the air all around him. A young girl, dressed in white, approached him and gave a demure little curtsy and held out her hand. He took it and she drew him into the throng of young people. Together they danced through the water. Jamie could feel the water splashing on to his head and body but his skin and clothes remained dry. He wanted to ask his partner why this happened but as soon as he looked into her eyes and prepared to pose his question the words failed to come and he forgot his question. They held hands and skipped around the fountain, Jamie grasped her round the waist and spun her gaily through the air. She was as light as a fairy.

As his limbs tired he moved away from the water and together they sat on the soft grass. He looked into her blue green eyes; hc had never seen anyone so beautiful. He was frightened to speak in case she should disappear. There were so many things he would like to know. The young girl read the questions in his eyes and she asked, "What name do you bring?"

Jamie thought it a strange way to ask but he politely replied, "Jamie."

"I brought the name of Voirrey," said his companion.

"That is a lovely name," said Jamie. "I have not heard it before. Did your mother choose that name?"

"I know not, I brought it just as you brought yours," was the reply.

They were still holding hands and Voirrey looked at Jamie's workworn fingers and damaged nails. They contrasted so vividly with her own delicate white hands and well tended nails.

"You have just come?" she queried.

"Yes," said Jamie. He tried to remember their cottage outside the castle walls but his memory was vague and, when he tried to speak, words would not come. He could remember being in the passage with a fishing line of fine linen in his hand, but his past was disappearing.

Eventually some words came to his lips and he asked Voirrey the name of this land and who were these people who danced and were so happy.

Voirrey hesitated to reply but then she explained that this was the land of the Gonaways. They were all Gonaways, and in response to further questioning she explained that it is ruled by the elders who were the first Gonaways.

"Are they very old?" asked Jamie, but Voirrey could not understand. She simply repeated, "They are the elders, the first."

Now that Jamie had started asking questions he found that words were coming more easily but he probed gently as he didn't want to hurt his new-found friend. When he asked about work, Voirrey was completely confused. It seemed there was no work, all was pleasure. They danced and laughed and splashed through the water. Night and day did not register either. They rested and they wakened, and all was pleasure.

"But you must have a special friend," said Jamie, "you know a boy-friend?"

"You are my friend," said Voirre, "We are all friends, there are no special friends."

Jamie tried to find words to explain. "But if you get a special friend, a boy-friend, then you can marry and have children. You will have a baby all of your own."

For the first time the happy smile faded from Voirrey's face. "You speak of strange things, Jamie. I have many friends, we are all friends. What is baby? Why do I want one all of my own?"

Jamie's brain was becoming confused. He had said that and now he couldn't remember what a baby was. All he could see was a beautiful girl with a mystified expression. He put his arm gently round her shoulders and drew her to him, "Do not worry, we are friends, special friends," he said.

Voirrey felt that this was something different. She sensed a new experience and she was content to lie close to Jamie. They were friends, special friends.

Jamie knew that they had passed through many periods of rest and wakefulness but time had lost all meaning. He had found happiness in just sitting on the grass or frollicking though the water with Voirrey always by his side. Voirrey also seemed to have found a new kind of happiness. She had a different feeling in her body, she wanted no one else to touch Jamie. She led him back to the spot where they had first met, where she had reached out her hand and Jamie had dropped his reel of linen thread and danced with her.

The reel was still there. Jamie took it in his hand and it stirred special memories. He remembered the dark passage and in his mind he created a picture of blue sea and a small ketch. He had a strange longing to see the sea, the sky and the sun. He held Voirrey's hand and followed the fine linen thread.

They approached the first chamber and saw the lighted mansion but they kept well clear as if they were eloping. They crept round the edge of the great cavern, still holding the thread, and entered the dark passage that twisted its way to the castle. Not a word was spoken, Voirrey tightly gripped the hand of her special friend and went in search of a new kind of happiness. Jamie's mental pictures of the ketch and the blue sea were becoming more vivid.

The linen thread led them safely to the secret entrance and they stepped out of the darkness into the court of the castle; there they climbed the staircase to the first floor and then up the spiral staircase to the Lord's Dining Hall. Jamie had this uncontrollable urge to climb upwards, to reach the highest point where he could look out over the harbour, see the land stretching out to Langness and to show Voirrey the beauties of his Island home. He climbed on and as they reached the top he could feel Voirrey's hand gripping his like a steel claw. Above him was the clear blue sky. He looked through the battlements at the sea stretching to the horizon.

He approached the wall and looked down searching for the small grey cottage that he vaguely remembered as home. But the world was different. It was a strange town. There were more buildings, the nearby houses were of grey stone but round the fringes of the town were buildings of red brick with green or red roofs. Trimmed lawns and neat flowerbeds surrounded these new buildings. Hard grey roads wound their way through the collection of dwellings. There were no muddy lanes or rutted tracks. Strange carriages mysteriously moved without horses and the people wore strange clothes.

He looked with fear and amazement as a huge flying object, a million times larger than any bird, roared overhead, circled threateningly over the town and swooped low towards Derbyhaven. Gulls, rooks and flights of smaller birds fled in terror as this creature settled on the ground. Jamie looked to Voirrey for comfort but found that the pretty young girl had changed into a withered old crone, the delicate hand was now devoid of flesh and the clawlike grip was created by bare bones. Before his very eyes she was shrivelling like a dead flower in the blazing sun. Her white dress hung like a shroud over her ghostly skeleton and in a moment she had gone. A small pile of grey dust on the top step was all that remained of his new-found love.

Jamie looked towards the harbour, searching for his father's ketch. The *Manx Maid* must be there somewhere. But the harbour, too, was strange. Some small boats moved but no one pulled on the oars, solitary figures sat in the stern seats with the tiller in their hands and strange streams of white froth stretched from the stern of the boats and appeared to push the crafts forward.

He leaned forward searching for anything that he could recognise and then he felt himself falling. The hard grey streets were rushing up to meet him but then his vision blurred and he, like Voirrey, changed to dust. A gentle breeze swirled round the castle wall and the grey dust, that was Jamie, gently settled amid the few boats moored in the harbour.

Jamie is at rest now. He is at home and the old men of tomorrow will tell his story to the children who sit around their chairs. But Voirrey - the Lady in White - cannot rest. She is in a strange land. She does not know the way to the secret entrance so she can never return to the land from which she came. She is still in the castle and when the moon is full, the moon that never shines in the land of the Gonaways, she still wanders round the castle searching for Jamie and the new earthly feeling that she discovered which must have been love.

The Captain's Last Trip

OLD Tommy Quayle was still the Captain to the fishermen of Peel although he hadn't been to sea since his stroke three years ago. For many years he had been the accepted leader of the fishing fleet that sailed out of this quiet fishing town but he had handed over his boat to his only son Euan. Now the old man spent the daylight hours looking out of their cottage window, perched high on the headland, being cared for by Maureen, Euan's wife. He stared longingly at the fishing boats as each evening during the season they would wend their way from the harbour, round the breakwater and lose themselves in the open waters beyond.

It was just over a year since Maureen had come to the cottage as Euan's bride. Her petite figure and dark glossy hair contrasted with her husband's blond hair and manly stature that was reminiscent of the Vikings that had pillaged this coastline many hundreds of years before. She was only eighteen when she fell in love with Euan and from the start she knew that he would always be part of her life. She married this sofly spoken giant, who was ten years her senior, knowing that as the wife of a fisherman she would endure both physical and mental hardships. When catches were low there would be lean times and empty stomachs. When the seas were rough there would anguished waiting, praying for the safe return of his flimsy craft. As a fisherman's wife she accepted all these trials, her love was also strong enough for her to accept the responsibility of nursing and caring for the old man.

In the little family cottage she found contentment surrounded by the kind and gentle nature of both father and son. The love and respect that they had for each other had engulfed her and she thought of the old Captain as her father. She was not as shapely now as she was when she came as a bride, but her face had that radiant glow so characteristic of the contented expectant mother. As she tended the old man she often wondered if her Euan would ever be called Captain and, if they were blessed with a boy, if he in turn would inherit the title.

The herring season was short and the profits small, but with a smallholding, a cow and a few hens they could eke out a living the year round. Now all the work fell on the young folk, but even without going outside old Tommy could foretell the weather and the winds. His experience told them when and where to fish, when to plough or to sow, when a coming sunny spell would dry the hay or a pending snowstorm would call for the laying in of stores. His advice was always sound and was readily given to Euan and the other fishermen.

After a fine summer with good fishing, September turned cold and wet; the bay was throwing up numerous white caps as Euan and his father looked out of the window.

"It's going to be a rough one tonight boy," the old man mumbled. Since his stroke speech was difficult and he struggled to find the words he wanted.

"It's the equinox that brings the wind." He paused, making a special effort to form the words that were in his brain. Saliva drooled from the corner of his twisted lips. "There's a lot more to come yet, son."

"Will it be fit to sail?" asked Euan. "The tide'll be right about six."

"Aye, safe enough if you're wise, lad. The wind'll blow hard from the rocks yonder." He tried to raise his arm to point but the movement spent itself before it reached his elbow and only two fingers twitched."

"Where do you reckon the herring will be tonight, Dad?"

"Off the south of the Island, about twenty miles out. They'll run to the north likely." The old man struggled to continue, determination written all over his face.

"Take care how you go, boy, and you'll have full nets."

The boat had to be prepared. There was always work to do and with half a gale blowing and worse to come, everything had to be right. Jamie pressed the old man's hand and then turned and gently enfolded Maureen in his arms.

"Take care, love. I'll be back before sun up. Sleep well."

A tender kiss and he was gone and she faced another long night of waiting and listening to the storm.

As the sun moved towards the west and the clock crept round towards six she was worriedly gazing out of the window watching for boats leaving the shelter of the harbour. The bay was a mass of tumbled waves; white breakers were rushing towards the shore and spray was flying in white clouds over the breakwater. Only the masthead was visible as a boat moved from the jetty at the harbour mouth but the Captain's sharp eyes had seen it.

"'*Neen Veg*," he mumbled. He had called his boat *Inneen Veg* - Little Girl - after the daughter they had sadly lost in her childhood.

The *Inneen Veg* tossed and rolled as she cleared the end of the jetty. Euan, with his crew of two, took his small lugger well clear of the breakwater as huge green waves rolled in and broke over the old but sturdy boat. The mainsail was set fine into the wind and the mizzen billowed slightly as the boat plunged ahead, receiving only feeble assistance from the old Petter engine. As Euan swung the tiller over to turn southwards, with the two crewmen handling the sails, the strengthening winds tautened the canvas. The boat scudded along and the younger crewman went below to cut the engine. Fuel cost money - the wind was free.

Everything was as the old Captain had said. The wind had gone round to the west and was blowing hard. The herring were where the old man had forecast. Euan knew that his nets were filling by the list on the boat; his only worry was the weather. The wind had matured into a full gale. It howled through the rigging and giant waves were breaking over the boat. His little vessel was alone. He had his riding lights up, but he had searched the seas and couldn't see the lights of any other fishermen. Both crewmen were fully occupied trying to hold the tiller as the lugger floundered from wave to wave, with just the mizzen up to give her a bit of way and hold her into the wind.

Euan was watching his nets as they tugged at the ropes straining over the gunnels. He knew there was no hope of hauling those nets aboard in this weather. He had never experienced gales like these and he was scared for the safety of the boat and its crew. His only thought was to get into the lee of the land, out of these terrifying seas. He would cut his nets free and run for shelter. With a few buoys on the nets they may stay afloat and perhaps, when the storm eased, he could come and collect them. If he lost his nets it would be sad and a hard winter and a lean start to next season.

"Oh Dad, why aren't you here?" he cried into the wind as the spray and the anguish forced tears out of his aching eyes. He tied floats to the securing ropes and then went below to get the axe that hung near the engine.

Coming back up he was amazed to see an oilskin clad figure examining the net ropes. He glanced towards the stern and saw the two crewmen still wrestling with the tiller. It's the storm, tiredness, worry and imagination he thought. I'm dreaming. He turned and looked again but the mysterious figure was still there.

He hesitated, he had to reach those ropes. He stepped forward with the axe raised.

His father's voice came out of the oilskins, but it was the voice of years past. There was no mumbling, no slurring of words. It was firm and decisive as it had been when Euan was a young schoolboy.

"No, Euan, no. Keep your nets, they're full. They're your sea anchor. Ride the storm and in a few hours it will ease. You'll be the only man with a catch. You'll get a good price."

Old Tommy had never made such a long speech since the day that he collapsed with a stroke. It couldn't really be happening, but Euan knew that it was his father's voice giving him advice even if he couldn't be there. Yet he was sure that it was his father who was bending over the ropes. Maybe it was imagination but the old man had always said, "I'll be with you in spirit, boy". There were strange tales told by fishermen and violent storms did odd things to people's senses, but he knew that his father had never given wrong advice.

He lowered the raised axe, turned and replaced it in the sling by the engine and when he looked again the strange figure had gone.

Euan rode to his nets all through the night. The old boat pitched and tossed but he felt safe. He and his two crewmen were wet, tired and hungry but they were still alive and he knew that it was the weight of his full nets that was saving them. With the dawn the storm lessened and by mid-morning they hauled their nets. Silver blue herring cascaded in shoals into the small hold amidships and spilled on to the surrounding deck. This was payment indeed for the discomfort and suffering of the past fifteen hours. With dark brown nets piled high over the mass of fish he set sail for Peel.

This was a tale to tell his children in years to come.

From before sunrise Maureen had been constantly peering out of the window; it had been a night of little sleep. She was willing that dark shape of a boat with brown sails to appear on the horizon. She had seen the lugger *Fortitude* being driven landwards by the strong westerly gale. She knew that the crew were fighting hard to get their boat into the lee of the breakwater but the ferocity of the gale had lessened only slightly; their struggle was in vain. In a last desperate effort the skipper had driven his boat hard on to the beach, hoping to protect the soft sides, but a huge wave had swung the little craft broadside and timbers had splintered leaving a gaping hole on the port side. She had watched the three men struggle ashore with ropes which, with the aid of nearby helpers, they had lashed to any solid object available. They hopefully prepared for a partial salvage when the storm abated and the tide ebbed.

The storm gradually weakened as the skies lightened. The bay was still stormy but the seas were now manageable. A good seaman and a sound boat could survive, but during the night it had been different. The wind had howled round their little cottage, ripping plants out of the garden and hurling them into the fields behind the house. Maureen had felt that her husband was safe, the Captain had said so, but she longed for his strong arms and gentle voice to give her comfort.

It was late afternoon when the *Inneen Veg*

entered harbour but Maureen had seen the tiny speck of a boat when it was still five or more miles out. She had glanced at the recumbent figure of her father-in-law and lovingly raised the blankets to cover his shoulders. She grabbed a coat and had run down to the harbour.

As the boat came alongside she had caught the rope and slipped it over the bollard to make her man and his boat safe. Despite the storm and the anguish of the night there was no sentimental greeting. Euan threw a string of freshly caught herring.

"With potatoes, for tea," he shouted. "Give me two hours."

Fishermen's wives don't argue. They know that the boat, the catch and the crew come before home comforts and personal feelings and all that mattered to Maureen was that her man was safe. She took the string of herrings and climbed the steep path to their smallholding. It was two hours later that Euan climbed the same little path. His tired and weather-beaten body filled the doorway of the cottage.

"Hello, love, where's Dad?" he said.

Maureen rushed forward, she took his salt encrusted hands in hers and looked into his tired eyes. She pressed her body close to his to both give and receive comfort. Tears of joy filled her eyes.

"Shush," she whispered, "the Captain's sleeping now, he's been out most of the night."

"What do you mean?" asked Euan. "How could he go out in that storm? He can hardly walk."

"But Euan, love, he did. Right at the height of the storm he stood up straight. 'I'm needed, lass,' he said, and he put on his oilskins without any help. I wanted to go with him but he wouldn't let me. He just said, 'I'm needed, but don't worry, I'll be back and Euan will too.' He walked towards the cliff and just disappeared in the darkness and the rain. It was terrible. I thought I had lost you both, but just before daybreak he came back. At first he looked just as he did before his stroke and then he sat on a chair and said, 'Help me into bed, lass, I'm tired but Euan is coming home.' I put him in bed.

"He's slept most of the time since then. I tried to feed him but he just mumbled his refusal. He looked so tired but at the same time he looked happy."

The young couple leaned over the old man's bed. Euan gripped the Captain's hand. "Thanks Dad,' he said.

He thought he felt some response but the hand was cold and when he released his grip it dropped lifelessly on to the bed. His father's eyes stared vacantly into space. Tears ran down Euan's cheeks as he gently closed those unseeing eyes.

Euan is called Captain now and he faces his tasks without qualms because he knows that the old Captain's spirit will always sail with the *Inneen Veg*.

The Phynodderee

THE auctioneer cast his eyes over the group of stolid farmers, most of whom he had known for many years. He was on an improvised platform and they were gathered round him in the open-sided Dutch barn at Ballanaquain.

"Now we're gathered here," he said, "to dispose of this property of Ballanaquain with all farm buildings, equipment, crops and livestock that was farmed by Captain Lefroy Bower-Jones up to his recent sad passing." His voice droned on regarding the Captain and his fine service in the South African war but many of those present needed no reminding of the Captain.

He had come to the Island some six years ago, having cleverly bought this farm under the noses of several hopeful prospective local buyers. From his first day he had had two favourite sayings, "Time is money, and efficiency means proficiency" and this had always jarred against the 'traa di lioor' (time enough) attitude of many of his neighbours. Despite this most were ready to admit that this come-over had the ability to farm satisfactorily and apparently make a reasonable profit.

He had looked at the big meadow and, to the consternation of the locals, had put it under the plough. Before the first furrow was ploughed his neighbour had told him that this was a fairy field and was almost sacred ground.

"Haven't y'seen the fairy ring in it, Captain? The L'il Folk dance there when the moon is full. Y'can't plough up their playground."

The Captain had laughed. "We don't have fairies where I come from, and if there were these Little Folk that you talk of I'm sure they'll be just as happy dancing in one of your fields."

He carried on with his ploughing and, in the spring, corn was sown. As the season developed, a fine crop of oats glistened in the sunshine and the Captain teased his neighbour about the Little Folk.

"I'll have the binder in there later this week," he said. "I'll take more per acre than any farm round here."

The moon was full the following night and a steady breeze swept in from the sea. In the morning the Captain gave orders for the binder to be hitched and harvesting to start. He strolled down to the field. His glorious crop was no longer standing erect, some lay this way, some that, and in the middle of the field was a huge ring of crumpled mangled corn as if thousands of feet had danced and frollicked all night through.

The crop was sacrificed but the Captain still insisted that sometime in the future he would once again plough and cultivate the fairy field.

He was a determined and stubborn man but his stubborness over the old road had more disasterous consequences. Weekly, following the pattern of his predeccessors, he would hitch the horse to the old float and trail round the side of the mountain to meet fellow farmers at the market, always complaining about the ridiculous waste of time making this journey.

"Why have I always been told to come right round the mountain?" he asked. "Isn't there an old road that runs over the top by the disused quarry? I'm sure it would be quicker."

Old Johnny Quiggin nodded. "Fair enough Captain," he said. "The old road is shorter, well it's just a lane really, but it's a nasty one that. Y'wouldn't be wantin' to go that way."

"Why ever not if it's shorter. It would save time and time is money."

"But there's a phynodderee on that road," said old Johnny. "By Gawd, it's a brave man that would drive over there especially if the mist is down or there's a touch of darkness. No, Captain, you had better stick to the good road round the mountain. What's another minute or two when you've got your whole life in front of you?"

"What's this phynodderee you talk of?" asked the Captain.

"Oh 'tis a frightening creature that you must always avoid. There's no friendliness at it at all, even the animals are scared and will run away. It's best not to go on that lane."

"More silly superstitions is it?" snorted the Captain. "You tried to frighten me off with your tales of fairies in the big meadow, I know the crop was ruined but that wasn't fairies, I'm convinced it was only a freak wind with eddies coming over the headland."

Willie Quayle had been listening to the conversation and offered a little advice. "What Johnny says is right, sir, but y've just got to be careful. Y're a stranger here and y' don't allus know the way of things. Maybe it was jus' the wind that dropped your corn, but it's better to be safe than sorry, an' I know a way round it. If y've still got the old horse that was bought with farm y' might be all right. The old horse, Mary, knew that lane well and could sense the spirits. She would only climb the hill if it was safe. Y'might try her sometime and see what happens."

The following week the Captain hitched old Mary to the float and slowly climbed the hill. The rate of progress was pathetically slow but the Captain persevered because he knew that it was still going to be quicker than the long road route. As the horse approached the old quarry it stopped and, despite the Captain tugging on the reins, it did a complete circle ending up facing in the same direction as it had started and then carried on at a faster pace over the cliff path to the market in the town.

There was a reception committee of farmers awaiting his arrival and the Captain knew that they were all agog to know what had happened and how he had responded. He was almost ashamed to admit that the old horse had been in charge and had refused to answer to his handling of the reins. But eventually he mentioned it to the other farmers. They didn't seem at all surprised.

"That's all right, old Mary knows best. She allus has a look round y'see. If it's safe she'll go but if it's not she'll be back home a lot faster than she came. If she sees it is safe - well she knows the way, just you let her have her head. When old Tommy had her he used to go to sleep and only woke up when she got him to market. The only spirits Johnny had were in a bottle under the seat. You can do the same, she'll look after you."

Right through the months ahead the Captain used old Mary and each week, as she slowly approached the quarry, she turned right round and then increased her speed as she followed the cliff path. The Captain fretted over the wasted time. The old horse moved so slowly and it had this stupid habit of turning right round. If only he had a younger, faster horse that didn't have foolish habits he was sure he could save a couple of hours every week.

He talked to the farmers about his problem but most of the old men stuck to the same advice to rely on old Mary. Only one voice didn't agree. Ewan Quirk had never been very friendly towards the Captain. Actually he had been hoping to buy Ballanaquain when it became vacant and had waited just a little while too long. He had been hoping for a lower price, although he knew it was well worth the asking price, when the Captain nipped in and got possession.

Ewan waited until the Captain was alone before he made his approach. "Y'know, Captain, y'right in what you say. Old Mary is a good old thing but she's had her day. It's time she was put down. I've got a young lively colt there that would just suit you. He needs a strong hand but you're an ex-cavalryman, you could handle him easy enough."

The Captain was interested and they talked horses. Two days later he saw the horse at Ewan's farm and was impressed. This was his sort of animal, a nice looking creature and a fast mover. Coming over the hill would be no trouble in future. A deal was struck. The next three trips over the hill were fast journeys with no foolish roundabouts and the Captain was well pleased.

The fourth trip was different. A light mist was settling on the hills and the sky was heavy and oppressive. As they reached the vicinity of the quarry, the sky darkened. A mysterious wind whistled round the cart, the horse's ears suddenly lay flat along its head as a horrible scream echoed round the rock face of the quarry. The horse turned its head and the Captain saw the fear in its eyes. He also turned and looked behind him and a monstrous being loomed over half the hillside. Strange pointed ears, large curved horns, a face of indescribable revulsion with a gaping mouth and fang-like teeth and glaring blood red eyes surmounted a grotesque body with outstretched clawing hands. The Captain shared the horse's fear and wielded his whip to escape from this fearsome creature. The young horse with a wild neigh plunged forward over the edge of the precipitous cliff face into the deep stony pit of the quarry.

The auctioneer's voice droned on; bidding was slow. The police said that they didn't know why the float had crashed over the quarry face. The magistrate stressed that the Captain was a very experienced horseman and was noted for his sober habits and never drank before the sun was at its height. Thoughts of the phynodderee were in the minds of most of the old superstitious farmers. Would the ghost of the Captain add to the horror of the area?

Ewan looked around, no one was making a move. He gave the auctioneer a slight nod and then - first, second, third - the hammer fell. Ewan was the new owner of Ballanaquain, and he'd got it cheap!!

Clagh Kerree, the Punishment Stone

"YOU'LL be all right now, you can go home. Where did you say you lived?" Mary looked vaguely at the nurse as she was ushered towards the blue van with barred windows. She was trying to search through her memory for details of her home. Slowly a mental picture was formed and she saw the remote country cottage that John and she had settled in when they got married.

"It's Lhergyrhenny, up above Sulby Glen. It's a lovely little place, so remote and peaceful, John and . . .", she stopped and shuddered as another memory came flooding back, ". . . we have lived there for five years."

The nurse gave an inconsequential shrug, "Well I don't think our driver will take you up there, but he can drop you off at Sulby and you can walk the rest of the way. Actually we're only obliged to take you to the nearest bus stop, but we like to be helpful. You should really have some company for a few days but that's up to you."

Mary climbed in and the van pulled away from the gaunt grey building which had shielded her from the world for the past few months. She couldn't remember when last she had seen her little cottage or the rough stone walls and green fields that surrounded it. All she could readily recall was a bedspace in that nursing home, hospital, loony-bin or whatever one called it, and before that an even more depressing prison cell.

The air was so fresh as she strolled up the glen that most of her worries seemed to disappear. She'd always liked walking in the wide open spaces and as soon as possible she left the road and headed across country to reach the cottage. She unlocked the door and stepped inside, into the relative gloom, and almost instinctively was going to call to John. Then she remembered John wasn't there any more. Unseen forces forced her to climb the stairs into the quaint little bedroom. Someone had tidied the room but Mary could see it as it had been when last she was there and as she sank into a chair all her energy and courage vanished.

Familiar objects were there but they weren't all in their right places - that stone, her Clagh Kerree with horrible brown stains, shouldn't be on the dressing table. Closing her eyes she could visualise the day she had collected that when she was just a little girl of eleven. Mum and Dad had always liked coming to the Isle of Man for their summer holiday and that year they had decided to visit as many archaeological sites as possible. Having investigated all the better known ones they were told that there was a grave of a warrior or king near the Starvey Road at Cronk-y-Voddy. So off they went to investigate with little Mary in attendance. When they had found the huge mound and created their own story about it they called for Mary and she had appeared with this strange looking stone. It was almost round with just one small flat surface but had the appearance of having been intentionally shaped.

"Where on earth did you get that?" her mother had asked. "You had better throw it away. You can't take that back to the boarding house in Douglas."

"But, Mum, it's a special stone, that strange little man gave it to me."

"What man, we haven't seen anyone round here."

"Well, I think he was a man. He was rather strange," said Mary. "One minute he wasn't there and then suddenly he appeared. He gave me the stone. He said it was a Clagh Kerree, a punishment stone, and that the man who was buried here used to have to carry it around as a punishment because he had done something wrong. I told him I hadn't done anything wrong so I shouldn't have the stone. But he said it was a charmed stone and, because I haven't done anything wrong, the stone will bring me luck and punish anyone who hurts me. He actually said destroy but I think he meant punish. That's what he said, so can I keep it?"

"But where is this man now?"

"Oh, he just seemed to vanish when you and Dad came along, but he left me the stone."

Mary had taken that stone back to her home in Manchester as a reminder of her lovely holiday in the Isle of Man and, years later, when she and John decided to get married and live in the Island the stone came back home. He had laughed at her childish insistence but Mary said that it had always looked after her and brought her luck; perhaps it had helped her to find John and happiness in this remote cottage which they had almost rebuilt. John had even erected a little shelf over the head of the bed to hold the Clagh Kerree. He had said it was nicely out of the way and not too obvious where there was no direct sunlight.

At first John had hoped that his writing would provide a satisfactory income but then he had found a part-time job in Ramsey. The regular wage was a big help but it had left Mary alone in the cottage for long hours. Despite this they had been happy days - but that was before she went for her walking and camping holiday in Scotland.

The holiday was a special treat provided by John. Mary hadn't even thought about it but John had suddenly suggested that she needed a change. Mary argued surely it was he who needed a change and a rest after working so hard. His part time job had developed into full time and often he was so busy that he would work late and be forced to spend the night in Ramsey rather than climb the steep slopes to their cottage. He knew that Mary had always longed for a camping holiday wandering over the hills in Scotland. He had said that he could look after himself for a couple of weeks; she must go and enjoy herself. Mary yielded.

She'd wandered over the mountains of

Scotland for a fortnight and she didn't need company amid such beauty. Her little tent and her bedroll provided her accommodation; her billy and small primus provided her meals. All too soon she was heading back for her own little cottage among the Manx hills.

These memories all flashed through her mind as she sat on that chair looking at the bed. It was the bed that had caused so much anguish and sorrow over the past months, but she would have to live with that.

She remembered coming back from that Scottish holiday and deciding to walk over the mountain from Douglas to Lhergyrhenny and to surprise John. He would probably still be at work but she had her own key. She had slipped it into the lock, but it didn't want to turn - the door was unlocked. John must be home - what a lovely surprise. She had called his name but got no answer, she climbed the stairs then, just as she had done today. Her brain had been full of the ideas she had for a special meal she would make for John to say thank you for allowing her to have such a wonderful holiday.

She had entered the bedroom and looked at the bed. John was there but he would not want anymore special meals. He was lying on the bed, naked apart from an unbuttoned pyjama jacket. The pillow and sheet were caked hard with dried blood. Mary threw herself on to the bed and took him in her arms. The back of his skull was smashed in and a blood-stained Clagh Kerree was on the bed. Her John was dead, John whom she loved so much, who had cheerily waved her off as the boat sailed and she had started her solo holiday. For days before, Mary had been planning and organising, arranging quick easy meals, helping as much as she could to tide him over his loneliness. Mary felt she owed John so much; he had worked so hard, often coming home late and tired and wanting nothing but to roll over and go to sleep.

The picture was so vivid in her mind. Her John was dead, cold, lifeless and bloodstained. She had automatically drawn the bedclothes over his naked body as if to bring some warmth into the corpse. Then her brain had functioned and she contacted the police. That was the start of her real nightmare. Questions, questions, questions, some gentle, some shouting. Clagh Kerree was held up, was thrust in front of her face, was gripped and beaten on the table.

"This is the rock that you used. Why? Why? Why?"

Everything seemed to centre round Clagh Kerree, the stone that had been treasured from childhood. The stone that would defend her against harm. She had loved her husband and she had loved that stone. How could they imagine that she would use one to destroy the other?

The loneliness of the prison cell had been almost a relief from people, press and questions until she had recalled that she was charged with murdering the one man in her life that she had really loved. She said again and again that she had been in Scotland and had returned to find her husband on the bed in an empty house. They asked her where she had stayed, who she had been with, had she any bus tickets, hotel receipts or other proof. She tried to explain that she had been camping alone but no one seemed to listen. She was taken for further questioning.

There were more people, new faces, but the questions were the same. She told them that John had persuaded her to go on holiday and that she had made preparations for his meals while she was away. She explained how she'd cleaned the house from top to bottom, washed and ironed and changed the beds with extra clean linen. They had written all these things down but they still had appeared unconvinced.

She had remained in that cell for days and all she could see was the body of John, smeared with blood, lying on the bed. Then they had called her for another interview with more new interrogators. The questions were more gentle and they pressed her about the bed, the bedclothes and the changing of the sheets. With a lady doctor present they had asked more intimate questions about the personal relationship between John and her, and even allowed their questions to delve into their married sex life. Mary was shy and embarrassed but for the first time they seemed to be listening to her as if they were believing her story. Then there were mysterious medical examinations and tests, and low- voiced discussions between the doctor and the questioners. Mary heard snatches of conversation - samples will be sent to England - odd letters DNA, - but then nothing, and a further remand for seven days. Before the week was out they had asked a few more questions about Scotland and then Mary was free.

In hospital they had told Mary that they had found her sitting in the Mooragh Park. She'd been sitting there for two days, but that was weeks previously. She could recall nothing of the stay in the park or the first five or six weeks that she'd been in hospital. But as time passed they had moved her from building to building, ward to ward, trying to revive her memory and rationalise her actions. Eventually they had said that she was well enough to go home and here she was sitting staring at the bed or the Clagh Kerree on the dressing table.

Mary knows now that John had a lover. They had worked together, often long into the night, usually in her bedroom. His overtime working and forced over-night stays had been a fictitious excuse to conceal the affair. As a special treat for Rachel, his new love, he had suggested Mary's holiday in Scotland and had brought his lover to share the marital bed at Lhergyrhenny. No one has put forward any logical reason why the lovers quarrelled. The papers say that she clubbed him to death with a large stone; it was found on the bed coated with blood and hair. Earlier they had inferred that it was Mary who had committed the crime but stains on the sheets had proved otherwise. Rachel has admitted that they were lovers and that they shared the bed on the fateful night, but she denies that she committed the crime.

She claims to know nothing of the stone, but that as they made love John's skull was suddenly split open and blood poured on the bedclothes. In terror she fled from the unseen attacker. Nobody believed her, just as no one had believed Mary and traces of her body fluids were found on the bedclothes. The jury didn't hestitate to find her guilty. Mary shuddered knowing the agonising loneliness of a prison cell.

As Mary's unpleasant daydreams ended she rose from the chair. The bed was made, the room was tidy, there was so little to do - only the bloodstained Clagh Kerree was in the wrong place. She picked it up, debating what to do with it. It had killed her husband - but how? She could throw it away, out of her life forever - but that would not bring back John. She recalled the strange little being that had given her the stone. Was he a man or a spirit? Had the stone some special magical powers? If she had been in bed would the mysterious attacker have struck her? For over a decade she had had that stone, it was part of her life, she would keep it. She would put it back on the shelf where she would not really see it.

She moved the chair nearer to the bed and stretched up with the stone in her hand and reached for the little shelf. She turned the stone to find the small flat section as she placed it in its old position. As she turned and stepped down from the chair the stone slowly rolled and fell off the shelf and buried itself in the pillow. Mary stared aghast at Clagh Kerree almost buried in the huge indentation and she heard the piping voice of that strange little man on that summer holiday long ago. His words came back so clearly.

"You have done no wrong, ineen veg, the Clagh Kerree is a punishment stone but for you it will be a lucky stone. It will protect you from harm. It will destroy the unfaithful."

HEADLINES

AS Mary drew the curtains, the street lights were flickering on and she glanced across at the *Chronicle* offices. It was Thursday evening, they would be busy planning the layout of the paper just as they had been on that Thursday evening twenty years ago when Mary saw the ghost.

The *Chronicle* was not one of those bustling mainland papers. It was a small paper in a small town on a small island. The compilation and production was a leisurely affair and the paper came on the streets every Friday afternoon. There was never any activity in the building after six o'clock, except on Thursday, when one or two of the more senior staff might stay until eight, putting the final touches to the impending edition.

Prior to seeing the ghost, Mary was the office cleaner, going in as soon as the offices were empty to give the place a good clean-up each evening. By seven o'clock normally, and nine on Thursdays, Mary had finished and the whole building was in darkness. She had never bothered to clean the old office because it was no longer used and, apart from some antiquated furniture that had been there for years, was only used as a dumping ground for any light portable article that someone wanted to lose. When the building was extended the architects must have forgotten this old room that could only be reached by climbing some rickety stairs at the end of the corridor.

It was on a Thursday night in 1960 that she saw the ghost. As usual, she had finished her cleaning about nine and had gone to the Victoria for a drink with her husband. It had been a perfectly ordinary evening with chatter and gossip and the time passed quickly so she had been surprised when the landlord called time. She instinctively looked down at her watch and realised that she must have left it in her overall pocket in the *Chronicle* offices. They unconcernedly walked back to get it, her husband staying outside while Mary went inside over familiar ground. As she passed the Editor's office she was surprised to see the desk light was on, but she was even more surprised to see a rotund little man studying something on the desk. She knew there was nothing on the desk apart from the final pull of tomorrow's front page; it was there when she dusted the office. It was always there on a Thursday night. She had seen it less than three hours ago. It meant that everything was ready to roll in the morning.

Mary knew everyone who worked in the offices but she had never seen this person before and yet somehow he had an air of authority that indicated his right to be there. In that fraction of a second that she looked at him he seemed to sense her presence. He turned, gave a happy chuckle, a half wave in acknowledgement, and moved away from the desk. He passed unhurriedly through the wall and into the corridor, up the rickety stairs and through the closed door into the old office. Mary didn't bother to collect her watch. Next day she wrote a letter and asked for her overall, her watch and the wages that were due to her. She hasn't been in the building since.

No one else admitted to ever having seen the ghost although some of the staff reluctantly confessed to having heard bumps and strange noises coming out of the old, and supposedly empty, offices if they had been working late. This often seemed to coincide with any delay to the presentation and acceptance of the final pull on a Thursday evening. Although no one was prepared to give any credibility to Mary's story, Harry Brown, the chairman, was concerned when he heard it. He called round to see Mary and produced old photographs of various functions, works outings and dances and asked Mary if she could identify the man she had seen in the office. The pictures were yellow with age but with no hesitation she picked out plump little James Brown, the long dead great-grandfather of Harry. The whole thing was a seven day wonder. It wasn't the sort of thing that the paper could publish as their main readership was of down-to-earth, God-fearing, countryfolk who didn't believe in ghosts. The management also discounted the story in the offices and works as they didn't want to lose any of their more nervous workpeople. Mary was helped to find another job; the ghost story died and time passed.

Business had not improved with time. The senior staff of the *Chronicle* were gathered in the boardroom. An older Harry Brown, chairman and managing director presided.

"Something has got to be done," he said. "If we continue our present downward spiral our doors will be shut in a month's time."

The editor and general manager took this as a personal attack.

"We have done everything possible for this paper, with the material and facilities we have we couldn't be expected to do better. I can assure you that it isn't because of excessive salaries that we are in our present position."

"Now steady on, Jack, I'm not getting at anyone," retorted the chairman, "it's just that somehow we have to sell more papers. If we sell more papers we get more advertising and that is what makes the profit. At present we're making a loss week after week. If we don't sell papers, people don't advertise. I'm looking for suggestions, not criticising."

Bernard, the print shop manager, who still wore his ink stained smock, butted in. "I always reckon it's good headlines what sell papers. Dammit, we haven't had a good headline since Father O'Malley was sued for paternity in 1968. Give us some good headlines and my lads can print as many papers as you can sell."

"There you go again," said the Editor, I write

the headlines, but I can't write the headlines without substance. If I get a decent story reported I'll write a good headline."

Chris Cole, formerly the chief but now the only reporter bristled. "That's right, pass the buck down to me. Hell, I can't make up stories, I can only give you what happens. Nothing ever happens in this little hole. Pinching stories from across the water is no help because the public watch it on the telly and then can read the story first hand in English papers. It was different years ago when the papers came from England by boat on a hit or miss basis. Anyway, locals want local news. In days past we were the only local paper and if anyone else tried to muscle in, the old man would run them out of business. Now we've got all sorts of opposition, free papers and God knows what."

Harry Brown let them bicker for a while but realising that it was a fruitless discussion, called them to order. "Come on, lads, it's no use blaming each other or the conditions. We've got to work with what we've got and work together." He paused, staring into space as if seeking inspiration. "If we could only get a good scoop just to let people know that we're still active, things could improve. I know things have changed but I can remember my grandfather banging the desk about the same thing when I was a boy. It was up in the old offic., He loved to quote his father as saying - we print the news we find and if we can't find it we'll make it - we could do with making some right now."

"Well," said the Editor, " I haven't much to choose from this week. Even the argument about the Royal Cinema has fallen flat. The Council want it down, the owner won't sell, it's just stalemate. How do I make headlines out of that. Anyway we're not getting anywhere. Let's get back to work with what we've got. It's Thursday, I want to see the final pull before I go home tonight and I'll make the best of it. I don't want to be here working all night, and I see the doctor in the morning so I may be a little late."

It was nearly ten o'clock when the Editor arrived at the office the following morning and the place was in turmoil. His office seemed to be full of people. Everyone was talking at once and the presses were not running.

"What the hell is the matter?" he shouted. "Get some of these bodies out of my office. Why aren't the presses rolling? It's Friday, there's a paper to get out."

Bernard, even more inky than usual, laid a paper on the desk in front of him. "There," he said, "that's the bloody matter! How did that happen? I saw the pull last night before I went home. The headline said - COW KILLED BY TRACTOR - but look at that - A RIGHT ROYAL BLAZE. There's a full bloody story about. It says that the cinema was burnt down. It gives all sorts of details but it's rubbish."

"Who wrote the story? Have you checked that?" asked the Editor. "And what about the cinema?"

"There's no by-line if that's what you mean," said Bernard. "Of course we've tried to check, but who do we check with. Anyway I came past the cinema at seven o'clock this morning and it was still standing looking as desolate as ever. You know, boss, we can't print that, it's pure fiction. But who the hell changed it? The whole of the front page has been reset, I'd have had to have a man working all night to do that. It'll take hours to change it back. We'll not get our paper out today, now. Who's going to tell Harry Brown? If we miss an issue it will finish the old *Chronicle.* You know what he was saying only yesterday."

"Get everyone out of here," snapped the Editor. "I can't think with all this rabble. Get Chris Cole and anyone else that you think can help. I'll get Harry Brown and we'll see what we can do, but for God's sake hold that front page. We'll have to find something easy to put on it."

Within half an hour the group of yesterday were once more sitting around the table, completely confused and bewildered by the striking, but fictitious, headline and main story. No one could offer any suggestions as to its origin. The final pull of the previous night had been innocuous but true; this was eye-catching but false.

Suddenly the quiet was shattered by the clanging of the fire engine's bell as it roared past the window. Chris Cole instinctively grabbed the phone and dialled a number.

"Where's the fire?" he asked.

There was a moment's silence and then the phone crackled as someone replied and Chris said, "It can't be. Are you sure?"

A rude retort caused Chris to hold the phone clear of his ear for a few seconds and then he meekly replied. "Sorry pal, I wasn't doubting you but . . ." Then having second thoughts he replaced the receiver and looked at Harry Brown. "You'll never believe this," he said. "The old Royal Cinema is blazing right now!"

There was a stunned silence and then the

Editor said; "Get out quick, Chris. Check that story. We've got the headline, by God. What a scoop! Make sure the story is right."

There was a sinister chuckle and then a sepuchral voice said, "O ye of little faith."

The team round the table didn't say anything but all eyes turned towards the old office. It sounded as if someone was banging the desk.

Mary had also heard the fire-engine and she learned from the evening paper that the old cinema had burned down. The report was quite extensive. Chris Cole read it with interest. It had his by-line but the words had been set in type before he had visited the scene and the words were not truly his, although the facts stated were exactly as he collected them when he dashed through the town in hot pursuit of the fire engine.

The report confirmed exactly what the Chief Superintendent had told him. The fire chief was convinced it was a case of arson but there was not a single clue to link the crime to any of the known bad boys. The police would continue their investigations and hoped to be able to give a full explanation of the fire in due course.

Harry Brown was a happy man. With more ink on his person and clothing than usual Bernard had produced an extra run and all were selling well. The Editor congratulated himself on his best headline ever and Chris's story earned him a few extra drinks in the Victoria. The old office was as quiet as a grave.

The Weaver

JOHN and Mary Kelly and their daughter Mona lived in a little white-washed cottage that clung to the slopes of Glen Auldyn. It was a very humble abode, just one room with a bed at one end, a loom at the other and a thatched roof covering it. The loom took a lot of the space but it was their livelihood. Their little vegetable patch and an old cow provided most of their food. They were poor, but they were happy together.

John was busy at his loom as Mona burst in through the cottage door. "Daddy, we've got to help her, she's a pretty little girl, just like a doll, and she seems to be hurt."

John looked up with an angry scowl. "How many times have I told you not to burst in like that. Now I've trapped my shuttle and I'll have an awful job to sort it out. Things are difficult enough with this aching arm of mine and working all hours without having extra work. You know I promised the gentry up at Ballakillingan that I would have this piece of cloth ready for tomorrow."

"Don't scold the child, dear, I'm sure she's got something special to tell us."

"I'm sorry, Dad, but this is something special. I was down near old Esther's cottage when I saw this lovely little creature crying."

"I've told you not to go near Esther's place. You know she's a witch and she'll put a spell on you as quick as looking."

"I know, I didn't really want to go down there but somehow I just went. Something was pulling me, and then I saw this little one. She's so pretty and she's crying. I think she's hurt but I felt I couldn't manage on my own so I came back for you or Mum. You're strong. You could pick her up and carry her. We could bring her back here and see what's the matter."

"Well, I don't suppose I'll get any peace until we do something, but how I'm going to get this piece of cloth finished I just don't know. Come on then, the sooner we go the sooner I'll be back," said her father, "But if I don't get this cloth delivered tomorrow there'll be no meat on the table for the next few weeks. It'll be naught but bread and jam. Come on, we'll all go."

In a few minutes they were following little tracks behind Esther's cottage.

"Keep quiet," said John, "I don't want that old witch catching us and weaving one of her spells."

They crept through the bushes and then they heard the stifled sobbing of the little creature who was hiding in the bushes. Mona was right. She was beautiful. John had never seen anyone so pretty. He bent over her and gently lifted her in his arms. She was as light as a fairy he thought; and then the thought materialised, I do believe she is a fairy.

"Are you hurt," he asked.

In a weak but gentle voice the little creature replied, "I was trying to help some of the poor creatures that the old lady has in her cottage, but she saw me. She's a witch and she cast a spell. Her magic wasn't strong enough to kill me but it has made me so weak. I just waited and hoped that some of my friends might find me. They sometimes dance in these fields at night, but Mona came and found me."

"You'll be all right now," said Mary. "John will carry you to our home and we will look after you until you are strong again."

When they entered the little cottage John went straight to the bed that they all three normally shared, "We'll let her rest there for now," he said. "I'll build up the fire so it will be a warm night; we can sleep on the floor with a coat or two over us. I think she needs the rest more than we do."

He went to his loom and looked at the broken threads. They didn't look as bad now as they had before and in minutes he had joined them up and started weaving. The cloth was perfect and there was no sign of the shuttle having been trapped in the warp. It would be a good piece of cloth and, when he was paid, Mary would have some money to buy food. He looked at the frail little creature on the bed and knew that she wouldn't be eating much.

It seemed strange just lying on the floor to

sleep but he, Mary and Mona cuddled up together and immediately dropped off to sleep and didn't stir until a wintry sun was shining through the window. John poked the peat fire to give a bit of life to the dead-looking embers and fed it with a few twigs to make a cheery blaze and Mary tended the stranger lying on their bed.

"There'll be no milk with your porridge this morning. I've used the last drop to mix with some honey for the little one. I had to feed her with a spoon she was so weak, but it'll do her good. We'll be quiet and let her rest all day, the milk and honey'll make her strong."

Mona looked at the little figure covered with the old grey blanket. "I think she's a fairy," she said. "Is she the one that brings me a penny when I lose a tooth?"

"Maybe," said her mother, "but keep quiet and let the little soul sleep peacefully."

They ate their breakfast in silence but then John sat back in his chair and said, "I don't know what you did with that porridge, Mary, but it tasted wonderful. I feel as if I've just had my best meal ever, and the tea - even without any milk - was lovely, it tasted like wine. I feel ready for a good day's work now."

"Yes," said Mary, "I feel the same. I think it's just the happiness that is in our hearts because we are caring for a poor creature that needed help. Well, you can carry on with your weaving and Mona can help me to wash these dishes."

John went to his loom and with the touch of an old craftsman ran his hand over the woven cloth. The suspected damage was invisible, the cloth was perfect. It was the finest piece of cloth that he had ever woven and it was almost finished. This was strange as he was sure that when he had left it last night there were still many yards to weave. He would be able to take this up to the big house this morning and he would have money in his pocket before nightfall. When he started weaving he found it so much easier to work, the pain in his right arm that had worried him for weeks had completely disappeared. Somehow he felt that his whole life had changed.

Before he could make any comment about this, Mary burst out excitedly, "John look at this. It's the old spoon that I used to feed the little one. Now it's all bright and shining, it looks like silver. We've never had a spoon like that in all our lives. It's lovely. We must keep it safe."

It should have been just another ordinary day but it was somehow different. The wintry sun outside had not enough heat to shift the hoar frost off the bushes but as it came through the window it had all the warmth and comfort of a midsummer sun. The fire in the hearth blazed happily although no more peat or sticks were put on for the whole day, but the most amazing thing had happened straight after breakfast when Mary had gone out to milk the old cow. Mona had quietly sat by the bed watching over her fairy.

Their cow was a poor old thing that struggled to give much more than a cupful of milk each morning, but there was no way they could afford to buy another one. But when Mary went to milk her, she noticed the bulging udder and she filled a big jug with milk and had to go back to the house for another jug.

"If we get this much milk we'll have to sell some," she said. "But for now we can have all sorts of nice things that will use up the milk. It will help Mona to grow big and strong and I can give the little one some more milk and honey."

John took his piece of woven cloth up to the big house at Ballakillingan and found the house full of people. They were having a party and were all dressed in fine garments but none of the cloths used in their clothing matched the quality of the piece that John had in his hands. They all gathered round to admire it and complimented John on his skill as a weaver. Before the day was out he had money in his pocket and orders from all the gentry for more cloth of this fine quality. There was going to be plenty of meat on his table for many months to come.

When the sun was getting low in the sky Mary said, "I'll give the little one some milk and honey and then she can settle for the night." She heated it gently in a saucepan on the fire and then, with the silver spoon gently fed the little creature and then tucked the blanket back round her as the fairy smiled her thanks. The three then settled once more on the floor with coats for covering and had an undisturbed night.

When morning came they stirred and Mona ran to the bed where her fairy had been sleeping, but the bed was empty.

"Oh Mummy, she's gone. I didn't want her to go, I wanted her to get strong and play with me."

"But, child, she couldn't do that. Don't you remember she said her friends sometimes danced in the fields near here, they must have come during the night and now she will have gone to join her own people."

Mary looked round their little cottage. It was all so tidy. It wasn't like that when she went to sleep. Bright clean curtains replaced the old soiled ones that had hung over the window. A colourful rug was spread in front of the fire, which was already blazing merrily. Then Mary looked at the table. It was covered with a shining white cloth and laden with all sorts of delicate china, silver cutlery and gleaming glassware. Three dishes were filled with steaming porridge and a huge jug of milk stood in the centre of the table surrounded by golden jars of honey.

When Mary went out to the cow she had another shock and dashed back to her husband.

"John, it's a miracle! The cow isn't an old cow any longer, it's a fine healthy looking beast and it's got a calf at its side. It's a bucket we'll need for the milk now, not a jug."

She knew that the fairy had gone home but the fairyfolk had said thank you for helping one of their kind.

John went to his loom. He had never seen such beautiful cloth and there were stacks of cloth all round his loom. He would have cloth for the gentry for years and years. No human hand had ever woven such fine fabric. He knew it was the work of the fairies.

John and Mary don't live in the cottage anymore. He has had a nice new house built with a special room for his loom. He always spends most of the day weaving but he knows that when he goes back to his loom in the morning there will lots of wonderful fairy fabric there as well. He doesn't have to go up to the big house to sell his cloth because it is known all over the Island and people come from far and wide to buy his special cloth. Every night before Mary and Mona go to bed they mix some milk and honey and leave the silver spoon just in case any of the fairy's friends are hungry.

John has bought the field where the fairies dance and will never let anyone plough it up or damage the beautiful ring that those tiny feet have worn in the grass. Sometimes at midnight a shy little fairy creeps into Mona's bedroom and takes her by the hand and leads her to the fairy ring. The fairies are all in thin white dresses and have silvery wings and they sparkle and shine in the moonlight. Mona joins in, dancing to the happy tones of the pipes that are played by little men in green jackets and pointed red hats. But she's always back in bed before her mother calls her in the morning.